WILD HORSE CREEK

# The Mystery Stallion

SHARON SIAMON

# The Mystery Stallion

Typeset by Roberta L. Melzl
Editor: Bobbie Chase

ISBN: 978-1-934983-10-2

Stabenfeldt, Inc.
225 Park Avenue South
New York, NY 10003
www.pony4kids.com

*Available exclusively through PONY.*

# Contents

# CHAPTER 1
# Rattlesnake

Liv Winchester shoved down her wide-brimmed hat and shivered with sheer joy. She was here at last — riding a high desert trail on a fabulous horse named Cactus Jack. Around her, the Arizona desert glowed in the late afternoon sun. Sun! At home in Vancouver it had rained for three weeks straight before they left. She'd been here a whole week and never seen a cloud.

"Hey Sophie!" Liv shouted ahead to her twin sister. "Isn't this perfect?"

Sophie turned in the saddle to glare at her. Liv could see that every line of her sister's slender body was tense, her dark eyes glazed with fear. "You know I hate heights," she howled. "Look where we have to go!"

Ahead, the trail became just a thin ledge across the face of the canyon wall. A towering red cliff soared above them and fell in a straight drop to a dry creek bed.

Wild Horse Creek! The name held magic for Liv. Somewhere, down there, where wild horses used to run free, was a small herd of Spanish horses belonging to her grandparents. Liv, Sophie and a whip-thin young cowboy named Shane Tripp had come to find them on this April afternoon and bring them back to the Lucky Star Ranch.

"You'll be all right, Sophie," Liv called. "Trust Shane."

The cowboy led the way, with his black and white dog, Tux, at his heels. Then came Sophie, with Liv riding at the back of the group. She held Cactus Jack's reins lightly in one hand, knowing her horse was smart and sure-footed.

❄ ❄ ❄ ❄ ❄

Shane's horse, Navajo, saw the snake first. It lay coiled on a flat rock right in his path. Navajo snorted, stopped and tried to take a backward step on the narrow ledge.

A shower of small stones skittered over the edge of the cliff.

"What's up?" Shane leaned forward to ask in the buckskin paint's ear. "You can't stop here!"

Behind Navajo, Sophie's horse, a white-faced sorrel called Cisco, jerked to a sudden halt. Sophie clutched her saddle horn to keep from pitching into the canyon below. "What's wrong?" she called anxiously.

"Keep still," he ordered. "There's a diamondback rattlesnake sunnin' itself on a rock. If you make a noise, you're gonna startle it. Good thing Navajo was smart enough not to step on that snake. Could have spooked the horses and sent us all over the edge."

"A *snake*!" Sophie shuddered at the vision of Cisco rearing, of falling over the edge of the cliff. She could see the rattler now, right in front of Navajo. It was dull brown against the rock, with pale diamonds outlined in white on its back.

"Keep your head up," she heard Shane talking to his horse. "Don't go sniffin' that feller and get bit on the nose. That'd be the end of you." He leaned over his shoulder to say to Sophie, "There's no room up here to turn the horses around. We're gonna have to sit here awhile and see if that snake moves on."

Sophie heard Liv crunch up behind her. "Why are we stopping?"

"There's a rattlesnake on a rock," Sophie hissed to her. "We're supposed to be quiet and wait for him to go away."

"Wow, a rattlesnake!" Liv leaned forward in the saddle to look. "Spring is supposed to be one of the best times to see one."

Sophie glanced back. Her twin sister, Olivia, though nobody ever called her that, glowed with excitement. Liv's brown eyes sparkled and two rosy spots shone on her cheeks.

"You're loving this, aren't you?" Sophie muttered.

"Hush!" Shane twisted to tell her. "And Tux," he spoke to his border collie, "Don't *you* get any ideas about goin' after that snake."

Tux whined and lay down under Navajo's belly,

with his paws on either side of his nose, staring at the snake.

As they sat for an hour with the sun beating down on them, it seemed to Sophie that the silence was pressing in on them. The only sounds were the cries of birds, the creak of saddle leather and the buzz of flies around the horses.

Then Tux, tired of lying still, gave a sharp bark.

"Hush you dumb dog!" Shane ordered.

The snake uncoiled, raising its thick, triangular head. Its tail stiffened. Now they could see the black and white bands and a row of rattles like small beads.

Tux barked again.

The rattlesnake rose up. Sophie could see the pupils of its eyes, like vertical slits. She saw Shane reach up and break off a branch from a dead pinion pine growing out of a crack in the cliff face.

"What are you doing?" Liv called from behind.

"I'm gonna try and nudge him with this stick," Shane said. "Get him to move on. Stay still!"

As he slipped from Navajo's back and swung out into space to stand on the ledge, the snake's rattle buzzed in the still dry air like the sound of bacon sizzling in a hot frying pan.

Shane poked gingerly at the snake. Its tail was moving so fast the rattles were just a blur. Its head was poised to strike.

"Hold your horses tight," Shane whispered to Sophie and Liv. "Don't let them startle now."

Sophie tightened her grip on Cisco's reins. "Easy, easy boy," she prayed.

At that second, Tux decided to take charge. Barking ferociously, the border collie dashed under Navajo and wriggled in front of Shane.

Shane threw himself forward, thrust the stick under the rattler in one swift motion and flipped it high in the air.

Sophie ducked in the saddle as the snake twisted above her and then it fell. She felt a sudden, stabbing pain in her leg, just above her ankle-high riding boot. The stick and the snake went spinning into space, down into the dark shadows of the canyon below.

Navajo tried to rear back. Shane leaped to his feet, grabbed his bridle and held him.

"Sophie!" Liv screamed, "Are you all right?"

"I ... don't think so," Sophie choked. "I think it bit me!"

# CHAPTER 2

# **Rough Ride**

"Where did it get you?" Shane stared at Sophie, his tanned face turning pale.

"On my leg, above my b-boot," she stammered. She was so frightened it was hard to get the words out. Her leg stung fiercely.

"Sophie ...," Shane took a deep breath. "Hold your leg as still as you can. We've got to get you down off this cliff." He pushed the cowboy hat back off his lean face. "You just hold onto Cisco and let him take you. Okay, now?"

"O-okay." Sophie nodded. She looked back wildly at Liv. Liv's brown eyes were wide and frightened.

"You're going to be all right," she said in a shaky voice. "Do you hear me, Sophie? You're going to be fine."

"That's easy for you to say! You didn't get bit by a rattlesnake!" Sophie flung the words in Liv's worried face. *It's always this way*, she thought furiously. If we go skiing, I fall. If we cut class, I get caught. If we have the flu, I throw up. Now we go riding in this horrible desert and I get a snakebite. Nothing ever happens to Liv.

Tux was still barking madly, looking down where the snake had disappeared. His harsh yips echoed from the opposite canyon wall. "Stop that noise!" Shane yelled at him. "You've caused enough trouble with your barking!" Clutching the border collie by the collar, he dragged him back from the cliff edge.

He swung up onto Navajo's saddle.

"Come on now, Sophie girl," he urged. "Along here a ways is a trail leadin' down to the creek. We'll stop as soon as it gets wider so I can take a look at your leg. Remember, keep it still as you can."

His horse stepped carefully over the rock where the snake had lain. Tux stopped to give it a good sniff, then scooted after Navajo. Sophie followed. She sat rigid in the saddle, her fear boiling inside her as Cisco crossed the ledge and rounded a corner of the cliff.

They started down a sickening series of switchback bends. Shane and Navajo were directly below her.

Cisco's hoofs slipped on the coarse sand. They lurched toward the cliff edge.

Sophie felt her stomach swirl. Everything went black in front of her eyes — she was going to faint! She gripped the saddle horn and squeezed her eyes shut.

✳ ✳ ✳ ✳ ✳

From behind, Liv watched Sophie sway dangerously in the saddle. This is my fault, she thought. I insisted that we take this high trail to Wild Horse Creek Canyon. I know how Sophie hates heights — back home in British Columbia she never skis the black diamond runs.

Cactus Jack seemed to sense Liv's misery and gave a reassuring nicker. He had a wide white blaze on his face, a white patch in the shape of a cactus on his flank and a kind disposition.

"Don't make excuses for me," Liv told the horse. "I should have listened to Sophie, for once!"

She remembered the day three weeks ago when her grandfather had called to ask if they could come and look after the Lucky Star Ranch while he took Gran to Tucson for some medical tests. "I'm sure it's just routine," their mother had explained. "Your grandparents aren't young anymore."

"I'd love to go!" Liv had danced around their dining room, flinging her arms wide.

But Sophie had groaned. "Why would you want to go to a ranch in the desert near a town called Rattlesnake Bend?" she'd asked, narrowing her eyes at Liv. "Just tell me, why?"

"They have horses," Liv had rolled her eyes at Sophie. "We love horses, remember? We've taken riding lessons for years!"

"But we don't know anything about ranching," Sophie had gone on. "What are we going to do on thousands of acres of Arizona desert?"

Their mother, Jess, had interrupted their argument. "Pop says there won't be anything to do with the cattle for the two weeks we're there. And you know you haven't seen the ranch since you were babies." She'd put one arm around each of her twins. "Let's give it a try."

"But our whole spring break ..." Sophie wailed.

"My folks need me," Jess had told them firmly, "and they'd like to see their grandchildren, so we're going."

Liv had wanted to visit her grandparents' ranch, the Lucky Star, as long as she could remember. But their family never went to Arizona, even though Gran and Granddad occasionally visited Vancouver. Liv asked her parents why they never visited, but they had always shrugged off her questions. And now they were here and the trip had turned into a nightmare. If anything happened to Sophie ...

She urged Cactus Jack forward.

※ ※ ※ ※ ※

Sophie heard Shane call, "There's some shade up ahead. Good place to stop."

She opened her eyes, expecting to see a grove of shady trees. But there were no trees. Instead the trail widened under a grim overhanging ledge of rock. They were still far from the bottom of the canyon.

Cisco stopped behind Navajo. Shane strode toward her. His eyes were a steady gray blue as he took her foot out of the stirrup and looked up at her. "First, I'll take off your boot in case your leg swells," he said. "You just sit as quiet as you can."

"Can I get off?" Sophie said. "I feel so dizzy."

"In a minute," Shane mumbled. He had stripped off her leather riding boot and sock and was gently rolling up her pant leg. "There!" he exclaimed. "Two puncture marks. Some bleedin'. And you're feelin' faint and sick." He shook his head.

"It hurts!" Sophie said. She wanted to get down off Cisco's back. Her whole body ached.

Shane squinted up at her from under his hat. "How bad?"

"You mean my leg? Not as bad as before."

"That's a good sign." Shane was still studying the marks of the snake's fangs. He whipped off his own red neck scarf, rolled it and tied it above the puncture marks. Then he tied Liv's below the two small holes. "If the snake injected venom, that'll help keep it from spreadin'," he said. "Now we're gonna get you off Cisco and you'll ride double with me. It's still a long way back to the Lucky Star Ranch."

"Lucky Star?" Sophie laughed hysterically. "That's so funny. I never have any luck except bad luck."

"Oh, Sophie!" Liv reached for her hand. "I'm sorry

we took that high trail. We might never have seen that snake."

"I'm sorry too," Sophie's laugh turned into a sob. "But right now, I just want to get off this horse, and away from this awful desert!"

She felt Shane's strong arms lifting her from Cisco's back. Gently, he hoisted her onto Navajo's saddle. "Same deal as before," he said. "Keep your leg as still as you can while we ride. We'll make the best speed we can back to the ranch."

He climbed carefully up behind her, wrapped one arm around her waist, and gathered Navajo's reins in the other. "Can you lead Cisco?" he asked Liv.

"I'll try."

"We never found Granddad's horses," Sophie suddenly said. She leaned against Shane as they headed down the final switchbacks with Liv riding ahead. "Weren't we supposed to bring them in?"

Shane nodded. "Your grandfather's worried something might happen to his stallion Diego, and the rest of the herd," he told her. "There are only thirty-five of the Starr-Lopez horses left, including Cisco and Cactus Jack. Mountain lions have been gettin' the foals, and your Granddad and Gran can't hunt the lions."

He paused. "We'll save lookin' for Diego for another day. But you might catch a glimpse of the horses down at the water hole along Wild Horse Creek."

"Okay." Sophie sighed. Shane was only sixteen, but

he seemed to know so much, to be so at home in this strange landscape. She shut her eyes on the steepest parts and let him and Navajo do the work.

Once they reached the floor of Wild Horse Creek Canyon the trail flattened out through stands of mesquite and live oak trees. Pillars of red rock rose on either side of them along the canyon walls to the west. Wild Horse Creek itself was just a bed of pale round stones winding along the canyon floor.

Sophie's mind drifted. The air was full of whizzing insects. Lizards scurried across their path. Cactus plants in strange shapes and thorny bushes caught at her jeans. Everything in this desert, she thought, had sharp spines or thorns, stung or prickled or bit like the rattlesnake.

"How much farther?" she asked Shane.

"It's not too far," he murmured in her ear. "Try to stay calm, that's the main thing."

Sophie could hear the worry behind Shane's soothing words. Was she going to die? Was this what it felt like — this strange whirling sensation? And so hot! Without the breeze that blew at higher elevations, Sophie felt as if all the life was being baked out of her.

Shane's thin, wiry arm was a comfort, and there were patches of shade where the air was cooler. Navajo blew and snorted to show his relief whenever they passed through a tree's shadow.

Liv had ridden a short distance ahead, leading Cisco. Sophie heard her scream, "Shane, look!"

"What now?" Sophie opened her eyes. Six large black birds had appeared overhead. They soared on widespread wings. Vultures. They were circling lower around the next bend in the dry creek bed. She shuddered, suddenly cold. Didn't vultures feed on dead bodies?

Tux ran ahead, barking. Shane clucked to Navajo and he picked up speed.

Around the next bend, lying on his side near a shallow water hole was a horse, a steel blue roan with a black mane and tail. Liv bent over him, her face twisted with shock.

*Diego?* Sophie thought with horror.

# CHAPTER 3
# Diego

"Is he ... dead?" Liv gasped. She could see that Diego was badly hurt. There was a bloody wound on his flank and another on his shoulder. The sand and rocks around him were stained red.

Liv felt a surge of pity. This was the great stallion whose pictures hung everywhere in the ranch house — in the hall, over the fireplace, on the bureau in their bedroom. All the pictures showed Diego in action, galloping, prancing, running with his mares like a king. Now he was lying here — like this!

Shane squatted by the stallion's body and took a pulse on his jaw. "He's torn up some," he muttered. "But he's alive."

Sophie slumped forward on Navajo's neck. "Is it really Diego? Grandfather's favorite horse?" she whispered.

Shane nodded. "Yep."

"Why doesn't he move?" Sophie moaned.

"Might have had a blow to the head that stunned him. Got to get him on his feet and get him to come with us." Shane stroked the stallion's thick neck and spoke in his ear. "Come on, Diego, get up, big boy."

A shudder ran through Diego's body. He lifted his head and then let it sink to the ground again.

"Those wounds —" Liv gulped. "Did a mountain lion do that?"

"Not a mountain lion," Shane shook his head. "A lion's claws and teeth don't leave marks like this." He glanced around. "I'd say he got into a fight with another stallion, but there aren't other stallions in this canyon."

He urged Diego again. "Come on, big fella. You got to come with us, now!"

Diego groaned but didn't move.

"We'll have to leave him." Shane stood up. "Got to get Sophie to the ranch." He tilted back his cowboy hat and wiped his forehead with his shirt sleeve. "We're still an hour or more away."

A great blue heron that had been fishing in the water hole flapped into the sky. The sound was startling in the quiet canyon.

Shane glanced around the clearing, his eyes narrowed.

"What do you see?" called Sophie. "Is something coming? What is it? The ... thing that attacked Diego?"

"Nuthin's coming," Shane said quietly. "That's the trouble. Where's Diego's herd? His mares and foals? They ought to be around here."

He bent and stroked Diego between his ears. "Did somebody beat you up and run off with your family? Don't worry. We'll sort it out. You hold on till we come for you, you hear?"

He swung up behind Sophie and they set off down the creek bed.

Liv didn't look back at the horse and the circling vultures as she rode after Shane. They had stopped for too long. She hated to leave Diego but Sophie needed medical help. Now!

✳ ✳ ✳ ✳ ✳

Liv glanced at her watch as they reached the end of the canyon and left Wild Horse Creek behind. "It's almost six," she called to Shane. "I can't believe this is taking so long!" Their horses cast long shadows on the rough sandy road that led from the canyon to the ranch.

"We'll be there soon," Shane promised.

"I'm glad," Sophie murmured. "Mom's a nurse. She'll look after me."

"Sure she will." Shane gave Sophie a gentle squeeze. He had talked to her the whole way in the same voice he used to talk to his dog, but she didn't mind. It was one of the things she had liked about Shane from the first time she saw him — the way he'd ruffle Tux's ears and speak to him in a low, serious way.

"Where's Tux?" she asked, looking around. Usually the collie was right there, trotting along by Navajo's side.

Shane glanced back.

"Darn dog's run off again," he said. "I've tried to train him to stay with me, but he has a mind of his own."

"Will he be okay?" Sophie shivered. Suddenly everything seemed to be in danger — Diego, Tux — the whole desert was full of dangers.

"Don't worry about that fool dog. How are *you* feelin'?" Shane asked.

"I'm ..." Sophie settled back in the crook of Shane's arm. "I'm thirsty!"

"Can't let you drink," Shane said. "That's one thing I know about rattlesnake bites. Usually, out here in the desert you have to drink all the time, but not now. If you have to have surgery, you'll need an empty stomach."

"Surgery!"

"Don't think about it, now. Try to stay calm," Shane murmured in her ear.

Half an hour later, they reached the entrance to Lucky Star. Over the metal-barred gate, a board on two tall posts was carved with the Lucky Star brand, with a large L topped by a star.

Liv hopped off her horse and ran ahead to swing the

gate open and let Navajo through. "Go on," she shouted. "I'll shut it and catch up."

Once the gate was latched, Liv jumped on Cactus Jack, galloped past Shane and Sophie and across the ranch yard. At the wide veranda of the ranch house she threw herself off Jack's back. "Granddad!" she shouted, pounding across the plank floor. "Where's Mom?"

She collided with her grandfather coming through the screen door. Ted Starr was a tall man in white shirt, black jeans and cowboy boots. The silver belt buckle at his waist matched the silvery gray of his hair and the long mustache that hid his top lip.

"Quiet," he hushed her. "I don't want you to wake your grandmother. I just got her to fall asleep." He stepped out on the veranda. "Your mother's gone to Rattlesnake Bend for groceries."

"Mom's gone?" Liv threw up her arms. "That's awful!" she gasped. "Sophie got bit by a rattlesnake! And Diego ... he's hurt. We left him by the water hole!"

Her grandfather's moustache seemed to droop farther down the sides of his mouth at her news. His face turned red. "Blast!" the word burst from his lips. "Where's your sister?"

Liv pointed. Navajo was coming slowly toward them with Sophie and Shane.

Ted Starr crossed the veranda in one stride. "Don't tell your Grandma!" He flung the words over his shoulder at

Liv. "You get those horses unsaddled and let them loose in the corral. Make sure they have water!"

Liv opened her mouth to protest — she wanted to be with Sophie — but the flash in her grandfather's eye made her run to obey him.

✳ ✳ ✳ ✳ ✳

Meanwhile, Tux sped back to the water hole along Wild Horse Creek, running low to the ground and as fast as only a young border collie can run. He pranced around the stallion's head, touched noses with Diego and barked a sharp order, "Get up!"

Diego opened his eyes. They were dull with pain. He struggled to his knees, then his feet, shaking his big head as if to clear it.

Tux trotted toward the water hole with his tail wagging. Diego stumbled after him. Blood seeped from the wound on his shoulder.

Long grass surrounded the spring, a vivid green against the desert brown. The edge was muddy and Diego's hooves sank out of sight as he poked his nose uncertainly toward the water. Finally, Diego sank his long muzzle in the cool water and paused to rest, before drinking in long noisy slurps. Next to him, Tux put his black nose in the water and lapped eagerly.

✳ ✳ ✳ ✳ ✳

"Bring Sophie in the house!" Ted Starr's voice was harsh. "In the living room, Shane."

Shane gently lifted her from Navajo's back and carried her up the veranda steps.

"I'm too heavy," Sophie murmured with her arms around his neck.

"You're nuthin' to lift," Shane said. He carried her through the veranda door and laid her on the big cowhide sofa. He covered her with a brightly striped Mexican serape from the back of the couch and put a big cushion behind her head. "Got to keep your leg lower than your heart," he explained.

"That's right, son." Ted bent stiffly over Sophie's leg. "Get me my readin' glasses from the desk," he said, "and turn on that lamp. I don't see too well."

Sophie wondered how he could need more light. The setting sun beamed through the windows to the west, shone on the dark red Mexican tile floor, the yellow stucco walls and the warm wood furniture.

"I wish your blasted mother was here." Her grandfather paced the floor. "Why she had to go to town again, I don't know. You've only been here six days and she's been to town three times. Sandra and I generally only go once a week, at most." He glanced at the closed door to his wife's bedroom. "Don't want her knowin' what's goin' on here," he said to Sophie. "So try not to cry out if you can help it."

"Is it ... going to hurt?" Sophie asked breathlessly. She'd heard of people cutting into snake bites with a knife to suck out the poison.

"Not too much." Her grandfather dragged a chair over to the sofa and sat down. "I'm going to take your other boot off now. Shane, go and get a basin of water and some soap and a clean cloth — and there's a snake bite kit on the top shelf of the bathroom cupboard. Bring that, too."

Sophie gripped the sofa cushion. Great! He hadn't said anything about a knife!

# CHAPTER 4
# Left Behind

In the corral behind the barn, Liv sped through unsaddling Navajo, Cisco and Cactus Jack with trembling fingers. What was happening in the ranch house? *Sophie needs me*, she thought. Whenever she's in trouble she gets all panicky if I'm not there to tell her it will be all right.

She turned the horses loose in the corral and watched them stroll toward a heap of scattered hay as if they didn't have a care in the world. They were beautiful with the slanted sun's rays shining on their coats, but for once, Liv didn't stop to admire them. She checked to see that there was water in the trough and headed back toward the house at a run. As she raced across the ranch yard, a silver van trailing a huge cloud of dust rolled up and braked beside her.

"Mom!" Liv choked.

"Give me a hand with these groceries?" her slim, dark-haired mother called from the open car window.

Liv blurted out the bad news as Jess stepped from the car. She watched her mother's knees crumple like the paper bag she clutched to her chest.

"Where is she?" Jess asked.

"In there, with Granddad and Shane." Liv pointed to the house. "Gran's asleep."

"Take these." Jess thrust the bag of groceries at Liv, "and get the rest of the bags from the car. There's ice cream in one." She sped toward the door.

*Who cares if a little ice cream melts*? Liv wanted to scream after her mother. Why was everybody sending her off to do chores? Nobody cared how she was feeling — that it was her twin sister lying in there with a rattlesnake bite. She should be in there, holding Sophie's hand!

She grabbed all four bags and staggered into the house. Sophie was already in her mother's arms and both of them were crying. Liv plunked the groceries on her grandfather's desk and started for the sofa.

But in the next second Liv watched her mother transform from a mom to a medical professional. Jess stood up, wiped the tears from her face and looked from her father to Shane. "What have you done so far?" she asked them briskly. "No liquid, I hope, or food."

"No ma'am," Shane said. "She hasn't drank anything since the snake bite."

Her father sighed tiredly. "We've kept her quiet and warm, and cleaned her up a bit — that's all." He yanked back a clean sheet from Sophie's leg so Jess could inspect it.

"There's the two puncture marks," he said, "but there's no swelling — her right leg and foot's the same size as her left. Her skin's not turning purple and black, and she says it's not hurting as bad as it was." He pulled at his mustache. "I'm pretty sure it's a dry bite — no venom."

"Is that possible, Pop?" Jess raised her eyebrows.

Liv came closer. The marks on Sophie's leg made her knees feel weak. Two small holes. Dull red.

"Sure it's possible," her grandfather told Jess. "I 'bin bit three times by diamondback rattlesnakes and one of those bites was dry. The thing is, if there's venom, the pain doesn't go away — it gets worse. And she'd be starting to swell by now." He put his large hand on Jess's shoulder. "But you're the nurse, and you've got better eyes than mine. You check her out."

"See," Liv crumpled to her knees beside the sofa. "I told you it was going to be fine."

Sophie's face was white and scared. Her fine hair stood out around her face like a dark halo. "But what if there is ... venom? Will you have to cut my leg and suck it out? Will I die?"

"Not a chance," Jess said firmly. "And they don't

recommend trying to suck out the poison anymore. Liv, go and get my nursing bag from my room."

Liv clambered to her feet.

"And then all of you clear out so I can examine Sophie." Jess ordered. She pointed to the forgotten grocery bags on the desk. "Liv — I asked you to put that food away."

"I'll *do* it, Mom," Liv said, running up the stairs to get her mother's bag.

She could hear her grandfather's deep voice from the living room, "If you don't need Shane and me, I have to go look for my horse..."

Liv snatched her mother's black bag from the dresser and rocketed down the stairs. "Wait! I want to come. I want to come with you to find Diego."

"What's this about?" Jess stared at her father.

"According to these youngsters, Diego's lying out there hurt, by the water hole," Ted explained. "We got to find him before dark."

"Pop!" Jess exploded. "We've got enough on our plate without you riding off looking for a horse! I should probably take Sophie to the clinic in Rattlesnake Bend tonight — I'll know more after I examine her — and we have to drive to Tucson tomorrow with Mom. This is too much for you!" She looked wildly from one of them to another. "Can't Shane go by himself?"

"Diego is my horse," Ted Starr said. "I'm goin' after him. Let's go, Shane." He headed to the door and then glanced back at Jess. "You don't know what's too much for me," he said.

Jess looked helplessly after their retreating backs.

"Mom?" Liv pleaded. "Can I go?"

"Don't be ridiculous — I need you here." Her mother opened her black bag and reached for her stethoscope. "They'll be riding hard — too hard." She shook her head. "I'm worried about Pop and someone has to stay with your grandmother if I take Sophie to the clinic."

She turned back to Sophie. "Do you feel any numbness in your leg?"

Sophie shook her head.

"Are you dizzy?"

"I was, but that was when we were up on that terrible ledge. It's better now."

"Your pulse is normal," Jess said a few minutes later. "And you don't have a fever. I'm ninety-nine percent sure you're fine, but I'd feel better if a doctor with some experience with snake bites had a look at you."

✳ ✳ ✳ ✳ ✳

After her mother and Sophie had left for the clinic in Rattlesnake Bend, Liv put the groceries away in the kitchen and wandered back into the living room. The light was growing dim so she switched on a table lamp. A photograph of her grandfather and Diego stood on the table. Liv picked it up.

"Your Granddad looks good on that horse, doesn't he?" she heard a quiet voice behind her.

She wheeled around. "Gran! You're awake."

"I thought I could lie on the couch and talk to you." Sandra Starr was a small, gray-haired woman with a deeply tanned and lined face, but her movements were light and brisk. "I'm sorry your mother wouldn't let you go with Ted and Shane. She worries too much."

"You heard?" Liv gaped at her.

"Pretty hard not to," Sandra said. "I'm a little under the weather, but I'm not deaf." She stretched out on the sofa with the pillows behind her head.

"Those tests you have to get done ..." Liv began.

"Just routine — nothing to worry about." Sandra pulled the serape around her. "Your mother has tried to spare me her troubles." She stopped and her blue eyes were very bright. "But I hear things. For instance, that your mother and father have separated. That's why you were able to visit the ranch. Is that right?"

Liv nodded miserably. "Dad moved out in December," she said. "Mark went to live with him and ... um ... Dad's girlfriend."

"That's too bad." Liv's gran smiled gently, "but these things happen." She paused. "Your brother Mark is the same age as Shane, isn't he?"

Liv nodded. Thinking about her big brother made her heart ache. He was probably skiing right now, staying at Whistler Mountain for the whole spring break. They would have been there too, if they hadn't come to Arizona.

Her grandmother went on, "I'm so glad you and Jess and your sister are here if I have to leave for a few days." She laughed softly. "I guess I'm superstitious. I believe there should always be a Lopez woman here on the Lucky Star Ranch."

*A Lopez woman?* "What do you mean, Gran?" Liv asked, leaning forward.

Her grandmother grinned. The smile gathered all the wrinkles on her face into laugh lines around her mouth and eyes. It made her look younger. She said, "My great grandmother, Maria Lopez, was the first. She came here from Mexico."

"That's why Shane called Diego's herd, 'the Starr-Lopez horses'," Liv breathed.

"That's right." Her grandmother nodded. "Originally, the horses came from Mexico. I, myself am one-quarter Mexican. Your mom, and you girls, inherited your dark eyes and hair from Maria Lopez. Her hair was heavy like yours, not fine like Sophie's."

Liv stared at herself in the large mirror over the couch. This was exciting! She swooped back her long, straight hair and studied her face with its high cheekbones. Sophie looked a lot like her, except that, as Gran said, her fine hair was always escaping from her ponytail in curly tendrils, and she was shorter, and her nose was much nicer, and her teeth were straighter. The truth is, she thought, Sophie is much prettier than I am.

At that moment, Gran reached up for Liv's hand and

gripped it with a strength that surprised her. She glanced down. Her grandmother's face wore a look of steely determination. "Promise me you'll look after my horses while we're gone," Gran said. "Diego and his herd are the last of the Spanish horses that came to this place with Maria Lopez over a hundred years ago. They are the soul of this ranch. If they go, it will all disappear."

*Had Gran heard about Diego, too?* Liv wondered. Did she know that right now, he was lying wounded near Wild Horse Creek. That his mares and foals were missing?

"I ... promise, Gran," Liv said, but she had no idea how she was going to do it.

# CHAPTER 5
# **Dry Bite**

Liv prowled the ranch house impatiently, brought a drink to her grandmother and helped her find a book to take to Tucson in case they had long waits in the doctors' offices. She dumped the basin of water out in the kitchen and hung up the wet cloth they'd used to swab Sophie's puncture wounds.

"I can see you're anxious about your sister," Sandra said finally. "Go to the gate and see if anyone's coming."

"Thanks, Gran!" Liv ran to the door.

"You won't need a flashlight," her grandmother went on. "The moon will soon be up. But don't go past the gate," she warned with a smile. "If your mother comes back and you're wandering around the desert on foot, we'll both be in trouble."

"I won't," Liv promised. It felt good to be finally doing something.

A few minutes later, she hung on the gate in the moonlight, listening to the singing of crickets and the sighing of the wind in the live oak trees. It sounded a bit like the ocean. Far away, a yip-yip-yipping made a shiver run down her back. That must be coyotes — barking at the moon.

Then she heard another yip, but this time much closer. *That's no coyote*, Liv thought. *That sounds like Tux!*

Soon she could hear the sound of hoofbeats clopping down the sandy road. Horses!

She climbed the gate, straining to see through the dim light. The shapes of two men on horseback were coming slowly, and with them a third horse, head down, limping.

"Shane!" Liv shouted. "Granddad! Is that you?"

In the next minute Tux bounced up to the gate, tail wagging like a victory flag. Liv hopped down, unlatched the gate and swung it wide.

"We met Tux coming out of the canyon, herding Diego in front of him," Shane called, slipping from his saddle to help Liv shut the gate after all the horses were through. "He must have thought it was his job to bring him in."

"What a good herding dog!" Liv squatted down to

grab the border collie and hug all the wiggly parts of him. "And I'll bet you barked at those ugly vultures, too, and scared them away!"

Tux licked her face.

"Let's get Diego in the barn." That was her grandfather's voice, and he was sounding very tired. "I don't want him runnin' off and lookin' for his mares. He can jump any fence on this ranch."

But as Liv watched Diego stagger through the gate, she didn't think he'd be jumping fences tonight. He limped to the barn with his head down, lip drooping, exhausted.

They put him in a little-used box stall that had cobwebs in the corners and smelled of old hay. "How can I help?" Liv asked. She felt so sorry for Diego — there must be something she could do.

"We'll get him cleaned up, fed and watered and see if we need to call the vet." Her grandfather handed her a bucket from the stall. He wiped his tired forehead with the back of his hand. "You can go get this filled over there." He pointed to a nearby tap.

While she filled the bucket, Liv heard her grandfather and Shane talking in low urgent voices.

"I'd like to kill the feller that hurt my horse," her Granddad growled. "Probably that Sam Regis from the next ranch. Wants the horses off the land so he'll have an excuse to say we're not usin' the spring. Then he can come in and steal my water."

"You think Sam Regis did this?" Shane shrugged. "Looks more to me like something bit chunks out of Diego."

"But what could bring him down?" Liv heard her grandfather ask. "You already said it weren't no lion. No wolves around here any more."

"I thought, maybe, another stallion?" Shane ventured.

"You mean my neighbor went and got a fighting stallion and put him out there in the canyon with Diego?"

"Could have been a wild one," Shane said.

"You're dreamin', son. There haven't been wild horses in these parts for over fifty years."

Liv carried the pail back to Diego's stall while Shane and her grandfather cleaned Diego's wounds.

"How is he?" Liv asked, handing the water to her grandfather.

He shook his head. "He's gonna need some lookin' after. I hate to leave my poor old horse with you kids — that is if your sister's okay and we're still goin' to Tucson tomorrow. Your mother insists she's gonna drive," he grunted. "Says my eyes aren't up to drivin' on the freeway anymore."

Liv said, "You could stay here, Granddad. I could go with Mom and Gran to her medical tests,"

"Nope." Ted took a large spotted red handkerchief out of his shirt pocket and blew his nose. "Can't do that. Sandra and I ain't been parted in forty-seven years. Not gonna start now — even for Diego."

"I'll help," Shane promised. "The girls and I will take good care of Diego till you get back."

"Thank you, son, but if you've got time to spare, Diego's mares need catchin' and bringin' home. I'm worried about them and so is Diego."

Diego lifted his head and snorted.

"Hear that? He knows what we're saying. Watch that he doesn't get out of this barn," Granddad warned. "Or banged up as he is, he'll be tryin' to jump a fence and run after that family of his and hurt himself even more."

＊ ＊ ＊ ＊ ＊

"There's a light in the barn," Jess said as she and Sophie drove into the ranch yard later that evening. "They must have brought Diego back."

"Can we go and see?" asked Sophie. Her leg still ached but it wasn't throbbing anymore. She had to find out what was happening to Diego.

"You go," her mother said wearily. "Tell Pop I'm fixing dinner and to come in twenty minutes. And ask if Shane wants to join us. It's almost nine-thirty. Everybody must be famished."

Sophie got out of the car and limped to the barn. A single bare bulb burned over a stall near the back. Liv and Shane were bending over Diego's right rear leg. Granddad was standing by his head.

Sophie felt a stab of envy at the sight of Liv's smooth dark head so close to Shane's. *How did Liv get along with guys so easily?* she wondered. *She never sounds shy or stupid when she talks to them.*

Shane straightened up at the sound of her footsteps.

"Sophie! What did the doc say?" Liv asked.

They all stared at her. She felt tongue-tied. "He said I was lucky. A glancing blow, that's what he called it. No venom. How's Diego?"

"Can't say." Her grandfather shook his gray head. "But I think I'd better call the vet, just in case."

"I'm sorry." Sophie tried not to look at the bloody wound on Diego's shoulder. "Uh ..." she stammered, "Mom's cooking dinner. She wants us to come in a few minutes and she wants to know if Shane is staying." She could feel herself blush. She knew it sounded as if she didn't want him to stay.

"Nah. I should get goin'," Shane mumbled, "when we finish here."

"Why don't you stay and eat?" Her grandfather came around Diego to give Shane's shoulder a rough pat. "Your dad's away, isn't he? You got no reason to go. I know you've got nuthin' over in that mobile of yours fit to eat."

"Thanks," Shane said. He gave an embarrassed shrug. "Sure glad that rattlesnake bite came to nuthin', Sophie. You can forget all about it now."

"Are you kidding? I'm never going to forget it!" Sophie tipped up her chin. *Or the way you looked after me*, she thought, remembering the feel of Shane's thin strong arm around her as they rode along Wild Horse Creek.

She was determined not to act so shy at dinner, and for once not let Liv do all the talking.

43

# CHAPTER 6

# Difference of Opinion

Jess had broiled huge juicy steaks, toasted garlic bread and whipped up a fresh salad. For dessert there was chocolate cake and ice cream. Candlelight flickered around the warm room and on the faces gathered around the round oak table in the ranch house dining room.

"Vet can't come till tomorrow," Ted grumbled between mouthfuls of steak. "He's over on the other side of the county."

"Try not to worry, dear. Just enjoy your dinner." His wife sat beside him.

Sophie noticed her grandmother wasn't eating much.

She wondered about Gran's tests tomorrow. Could there be something seriously wrong?

Shane, on the other hand, munched steak as if he hadn't eaten in days. Sophie studied his thin face, his tanned cheeks — the way the muscles in his jaw worked.

"Where do you live, Shane?" she asked.

Shane stopped chewing and swallowed. "Over the other side of the hill." He gestured out the window. "My dad and me have a mobile on a small plot."

"A mobile home? Like a trailer?" Liv looked up.

"Yep." Shane sawed himself another bite of steak. "An old Airstream."

"Does your dad just leave you there alone when he goes away?" Liv frowned.

"Yep," Shane said again. "He's in sales. Travels a lot. I want to finish school, so I got to stay put." He bent over his steak.

"Shane's a godsend to us," Sandra said. "Ted and I don't know what we'd do without his help. He works on the ranch after school and on the weekends."

"I'm glad you were here today," Sophie hugged herself. "What an awful day!"

Jess laughed. "The way I remember from when I was a kid on this ranch, it was pretty normal. Always some kind of a crisis around here. Mad bulls, dust storms, lost cattle, mountain lions." She passed the bread to her father. "Remember how you used to take me on the cattle roundups every spring and fall, Pop?"

"Sure do," he said. "Those were good days."

"Mom," Liv asked, as they were carrying the dinner plates to the big ranch kitchen that stretched across the back of the house, "how come we didn't visit Gran and Granddad here on the ranch when we were little kids?"

"I should have brought you and Sophie a long time ago." Jess put the plates on the kitchen counter and her arm around Liv. "I didn't because Pop and your father had a fight when we first got married, and your dad would never even talk about coming back."

"What did they fight about?" Sophie asked.

"Oh, your granddad didn't like George," Jess said. "He was a city guy and he'd taken me away to a city up north — to a different country. My parents always thought I'd marry a rancher and settle down here, and ...." She paused.

"And take over the Lucky Star Ranch?" Liv finished for her.

"I guess so." Jess sighed. "You girls give these plates a rinse and then we'll have dessert." She headed back to the dining room.

Liv dumped her plates in the sink and sloshed water on them. The water splashed high, wetting both her tee shirt and Sophie's.

"What's the matter with you?" Sophie asked, startled.

"I'm mad, that's what!" Liv muttered furiously. "Do you *realize* we could have been coming to this ranch our whole lives — every summer? I could have learned

46

to ride and round up cattle, instead of riding in a stupid indoor ring." She turned to glare at Sophie. "I could have had a horse of my own, a fabulous Spanish horse like Cactus Jack, instead of riding school horses! This —" She gestured around the kitchen with a dripping hand, " — this could all have been ours!"

Sophie rescued a dish that was sliding off the counter. "That fight must be part of the reason Dad hates this ranch. I'm glad he does. Otherwise we'd have spent every vacation here in this dry, horrible desert full of scorpions and crazy bulls and snakes. Always a crisis — you heard what Mom said about the ranch when she was young."

"I heard. Cattle roundups every spring and fall — it sounded great. You have no sense of adventure!" Liv flung the words at her.

"AND YOU HAVE NO IMAGINATION!" Sophie flung back. "At the clinic I saw pictures of what rattlesnake bites can do to you. Your flesh turns black and rots! Did you know that?"

They stood, glaring at each other.

"I'm sorry." Liv lowered her head. "I wish it had been *me* that got bit by that snake."

"It's never you," sighed Sophie. "But it's all right."

It's always like this with Liv, she thought as she finished rinsing the dishes. Liv and I disagree, flare up and fight, and then one of us gives in and we get along again. At least, up until now, it's worked that way. If only

47

Liv would realize that we're different! I don't always want to do all the crazy things she wants to do.

※ ※ ※ ※ ※

After cake and ice cream Shane left, riding off in the dark with Tux trotting after him.

Sophie and Liv watched them from the veranda until they disappeared. Heard the clop of Navajo's hoofs going down the gravel lane, a pause while Shane opened and shut the ranch gate. The hoof beats started again and finally faded in the distance. It was the loneliest sound Sophie had ever heard.

Shane was only three years older than she was — and he had to live alone. Since Mom and Dad split, Mark lived with Dad. When Dad traveled he must stay on his own, too.

"I miss Mark." Liv said, as if she could read Sophie's thoughts. She slumped into one of the big veranda chairs. "He'd love it here."

"No he wouldn't! He's probably skiing right now. Spring skiing — warm —"

"Foggy, rainy, slushy," Liv finished. "Can't even see the mountains most of the time."

"Do you like Shane?" Sophie plopped into another chair and changed the subject.

Liv shrugged. "Shane? Sure. He was fantastic up there on that ledge today, even if he did almost throw a snake on top of you." She grinned at Sophie, then gasped, "Oh! You mean do I *like him* like him? Why? Do you?"

Sophie could feel her twin's eyes on her. "I ... don't know." She suddenly didn't want to put her feelings for Shane into words.

"You're the one who's always saying we're too young for guys," Liv teased. "Has *Shane* changed your mind?"

"It's not like that!" Sophie stared off into the cool desert darkness. "Shane just seems ... older ... and like he really cares about things."

"He's more your type than mine," Liv said. She jumped up from her chair. "We should check on Diego. Coming?"

"No." Sophie shivered. "That poor horse looks awful with his head hanging down and his eyes sunk in. He looks like those skulls!" The cattle skulls nailed to the veranda posts on either side of the steps looked eerie in the yellow light from the ranch house windows. "Why do they put up those ugly things with their empty eye sockets and horrible sharp horns?"

"You're such a wuss!" Liv groaned. "Cattle skulls are a kind of symbol of the southwest, like totem poles in Vancouver, that's all. Stay here then. I'm going."

"You wouldn't think they were so cool if they were horse skulls," Sophie shot after her as Liv sped away toward the barn.

"Sophie?" She heard a voice call from an open window behind her. "Can you come here for a minute?"

"Sure, Gran." Sophie leaped out of her chair. That must be her grandmother's bedroom window. Had Gran heard their whole conversation?

Sandra was stretched out on the bed, dressed in her plaid flannel nightgown and moccasins. She patted the bed beside her.

Sophie sat down.

"I'm glad the snake bite came to nothing," her grandmother said. "But it must have been a frightening experience." She looked into Sophie's eyes as if she really knew how terrifying it had been.

"I don't like ..." Sophie started. She wanted to tell her grandmother how she didn't like snakes, or riding on high ledges or through thorn bushes, but her grandmother interrupted with a squeeze of her hand.

"I've already told Olivia, but I want you to know how happy I am that you came," she said softly.

Sophie didn't know what to say. Except for seeing Gran and Granddad, she wasn't even the smallest, tiniest bit happy she'd come!

"I hope you'll enjoy your time here," Sandra went on.

Sophie smothered a sigh. There were still seven endless days left.

"And one more thing." Gran's blue eyes bored into hers. "Where are you sleeping?"

"Upstairs," Sophie said, surprised, "with Liv."

Gran smiled at her. "While your grandfather and I are gone, why don't you move in here? I guess you haven't had your own room for a good while."

"Never!" The word burst from Sophie. It was true. She and Liv had shared a bedroom since the day they were born.

51

"Well, it's about time you had a little space of your own." Gran looked around the high-ceilinged bedroom. "This is a nice room."

"It's very nice," gulped Sophie. How did Gran know that some nights she pulled the covers over her head dreaming that she was somewhere far away from Liv's cheerful chatter?

There was no time to ask how she knew. Her mother was at the door, motioning her out. "Let Gran rest," she said. "Big day tomorrow."

Gran grinned and shook her head. Just like Liv, her eyes seemed to say, *She always thinks she knows what's good for you.*

"Think about what I said," she whispered, giving Sophie's hand a final squeeze.

# CHAPTER 7

# **Doctor Tux**

Gran and Granddad left before breakfast, with Jess driving the van.

Sophie was sorry to see her grandmother go. Gran talked to her as if she was a separate person, not just part of a blob called "the twins." After they'd gone, Sophie gathered her things and started downstairs to her grandparents' empty room.

Liv clattered down the stairs after her. "What are you doing?"

Sophie dumped her clothes on the big, neatly made bed. "Gran thought I might as well sleep in here."

Liv looked around the room with its high wood ceiling

and paneled walls. "Great idea. We'd be closer to the door if we need to go to Diego."

"Gran meant just me," Sophie muttered. She watched a stunned look come over her twin's face.

"Why?" Liv asked. "Why would you want to sleep in a different room?"

"Why not?" Sophie tried to keep her voice light. "We're not going to spend the rest of our lives sharing a bedroom."

"N-no. I guess not." Liv threw up her arms. "Okay. Try it out. See how you like it. You'll probably get scared all by yourself."

A dog was barking at the front door, and they turned together to see Shane banging the dust off his hat in the doorway and stepping shyly inside. "Tux — you stay out, boy," he ordered, and the dog sat obediently on the veranda, looking through the screen door, his tongue hanging out, panting.

"Oh, let him in," Liv laughed. "He's one of the family."

"Would you like some breakfast?" Sophie asked. "We were just going to make ours."

The conversation at breakfast was all about Diego and his lost mares. Shane didn't say much. Sophie noticed that he broke off little pieces of toast and bacon and fed them to Tux when he thought no one was looking.

"Where do you think you'll look for the herd?" Liv asked him.

Shane paused to swallow a mouthful of toast and jam. "I'll start by Wild Horse Creek, near the spring where we found Diego," he mumbled.

"I'm going with you," Liv announced, waving her bacon in the air. "I promised Gran I'd look after Diego's herd."

"What do you know about rounding up horses?" Sophie asked.

"Doesn't matter what I know," said Liv. "Cactus Jack will do all the work. Granddad said he's an amazing cow horse. Right, Shane?"

Shane gave a little grin. "You'll have to hold on tight," he warned. "Cow horses move pretty quick." He scraped his chair back, stood up and glanced at Sophie. "You should stay here and take it easy after yesterday," he said. "You can keep an eye on Diego till the vet comes."

Sophie wanted to protest — say she wanted to go with them. Instead she said, "Okay, but you'll have to show me what to do."

They trooped out to the barn.

Diego stood in his stall, head down. He blew softly as Tux reached up to touch noses.

Shane leaned over the stall door and stroked Diego's neck. "You haven't eaten much, old boy," he murmured. "Or had much water."

He showed Sophie the almost full water bucket and hay net. "Try to get him to eat and drink," he said, "and keep an eye on this wound on his shoulder. It feels a bit warm — might be starting an infection."

Sophie felt a ball of fear start to grow in her belly. "What do I do if he won't drink, or the infection gets worse?" she asked. She couldn't even look at Diego's shoulder wound. One glance was enough. It looked crusty and red.

"Don't worry too much. The vet'll be along some time this morning." Shane told her. "And I'll leave Tux here with you." He bent down to ruffle Tux's ears. "You watch this horse for me, hear?" he murmured. "You're as good for Diego as a vet, any day."

He shut Tux in Diego's stall. "Time to saddle up," he told Liv. "Got a canteen?"

"No." Liv shook her head. "Will we be gone that long?"

"Better take a couple of full canteens, and some grub, too, in case we're out there a while," Shane led the way out of the barn. "You never know."

"Okay, it'll just take a minute." Liv raced off toward the ranch house.

Sophie helped Shane saddle and bridle Cactus Jack while they waited. "I hope you're not gone too long," Sophie said as she did up Jack's bridle. The thought of a whole day spent by herself in this lonely place pressed down on her. Mom wouldn't be back till afternoon.

"We'll come back as soon as we can." Shane tightened Cactus Jack's cinch. He gave Sophie's shoulder a quick pat that reminded her of the way he patted Tux. "You just rest up. That was quite a shock you had yesterday."

Sophie glanced up at him. "It would have been much worse if it hadn't been for you," she said shyly.

"Are you kiddin'?" Shane gave an embarrassed laugh. "I was the guy that threw the snake at you, remember?" He stood looking down at her with laughter in his eyes. "I guess both of us will always remember that."

"Yes," said Sophie. "We will."

Shane reached out his hand again. He wanted to say something else, or maybe give her another awkward pat, Sophie thought, but at that moment Liv came climbing through the bars of the corral fence with a package of sandwiches and a canteen ready to stuff in Cactus Jack's saddlebag.

Sophie wished she were going instead of Liv. If she could just be alone with Shane for a whole day, she was sure they'd get to be good friends. Maybe more than friends. But the thought of a long ride through the desert, with steep trails and dust in her face, was totally unappealing.

After they'd gone, she turned back to the barn. Diego stood silently in his stall. Tux lay stretched out on the straw, his brown eyes fixed on the horse's face. He whined softly.

"I know you hate being left behind," she said to the dog. "Me too."

They both watched Diego. Every now and then a shudder ran through the stallion's body. He was suffering, poor thing. Sophie reached out her hand to him, trying to fight down her fear. Hurt as he was, he still gave off an aura of tremendous power and strength with his huge thick neck and powerful shoulders. You never knew when a horse like that would lash out and hurt somebody.

But Diego just blinked as she rubbed his forehead lightly. It was as though he didn't have the strength to respond.

"You have to hold on till the vet arrives — you hear me?" she whispered to him. "Come on, have some nice cool water." She held the bucket of water up to his head. Diego dipped his nose in the bucket but didn't drink.

Sophie dared herself to put her hand on his shoulder near the wound, and then drew it back suddenly. It was hot, just as she feared it might be.

"Oh, Diego," she groaned. "I wish they hadn't left us here alone with you. I don't know what to do!"

It felt weird, not having Liv offering suggestions. Even though they weren't identical twins, they shared a birthday and all the big life events: first day of kindergarten, first dentist appointment, first swimming lesson where you had to put your head underwater, first time buying a bra. Liv always faced challenges head on.

But there was no Liv to tell her how to help Diego, or to tell her everything would be all right. If only that vet would come!

✳ ✳ ✳ ✳ ✳

Hours later Sophie heard the purr of a big truck engine outside the barn. She raced to the barn door in time to see a red double-cab pickup roll into the ranch yard. She held her breath while two people got out of the cab.

# CHAPTER 8
# Visitors

They strode toward her. The girl was a vision. She
had a healthy glowing tan, perfect skin, tawny hair,
designer jeans and a fringed leather jacket that floated
around her as she moved. Every inch of her from hat
to white leather boots was decorated with turquoise
and silver. She looked more like a pop star than a
veterinarian.

"Hel-lo!" the girl said in surprise. "I'm Dayna, Dayna
Regis. I'm looking for Shane. Is he here?"

"Uh — no," Sophie stammered. Now that she was
up close Sophie could see that Dayna was not that much
older than herself — maybe sixteen or seventeen.

"Who are you?" Dayna was looking at her as if she was a strange object she'd discovered in her soup.

"I — I'm Sophie Winchester. The Starrs are my grandparents. Do you know them?"

"Of course I know them. We live on the next ranch. This is Temo Diaz. He works for us." The girl introduced the young man behind her with a careless wave of her hand.

He was the handsomest guy Sophie had ever seen — taller than Shane and broad through the shoulders. His hair was dark and cut close to his head, his eyes, nose and mouth perfect. He wore a shabby jean vest and dusty hat, but his clothes looked comfortable and lived-in compared to the glamour of the goddess in front of him.

Dayna was still staring at her. She slid her sunglasses down her nose for a better look. "You're so — pale!" she exclaimed. "Are you sick or something? Because we do great healing treatments at our spa." She pointed to a sign on the side of the truck. "Silver Spur Ranch — it's the best guest ranch and spa in the whole southwest."

"I'm not sick," Sophie said. "I'm from Vancouver. We don't get a lot of sun in April."

"Don't worry," Dayna said with another wave of her hand. "Twenty minutes in one of our tanning beds and you'll look normal."

"I'm not much into getting a tan."

"Your choice." Sophie could tell that Dayna had lost interest in her. "Do you know where Shane is? I want him to come over and look at a new horse I got."

"He — he's out looking for my grandparents' horses," Sophie explained.

Suddenly the girl's eyes widened and she looked very interested. She stepped closer, with the fringe on her jacket swinging. "Why? Are they lost?"

Should she say? Was it any of this girl's business? "We ... uh ... don't know," Sophie stammered.

"Then why is Shane looking for the herd?"

Sophie decided she had to trust them. Maybe they could help, if they were from a ranch. "Diego got hurt," she said quickly. "The other horses weren't with him when we found him. My mother's gone to Tucson with my grandparents, but — could you take a look? I don't know if he's getting worse or not."

"Sure," Dayna said. She swept past Sophie into the barn. Sophie tried to let Temo go ahead of her, but he hung back with a shrug.

"Go ahead," he said gesturing with his hand.

"All right." She smiled at him as she went through the door of the barn.

Inside, Dayna marched back to Diego's stall as if she owned the ranch. Tux growled low in his throat, but she ignored the border collie.

"Look Temo — the great Diego!" Dayna turned to Temo. "Just an ordinary horse, not a super stud like

61

everybody says. Wow! He's messed up pretty bad — wait till Daddy hears."

She sounds happy about it, Sophie thought, shocked.

"Poor *hombre*." Temo slipped into Diego's stall and spoke gently in his ear. The Spanish words were soft and musical.

"Let's go," Dayna said, turning away.

Temo rubbed Diego gently between the ears. "*Adiós, amigo*," he told Diego, backing slowly out of the stall.

Sophie shut Diego's stall with a bang. She wanted these two out of the barn. They couldn't help her, and that girl was somehow glad Diego was hurt.

"Tell Shane I'm looking for him," Dayna said as she swished past Sophie. "Dayna Regis. Can you remember that?"

"Clearly," said Sophie. She caught the glint of a grin on Temo's face as they climbed back in the truck. He leaned out his window to say, "Talk to the *manadero*. It will help him."

"Mind your own business," Dayna demanded. "It has nothing to do with us."

How can she be so rude to Temo? Sophie marveled. It was as though she was used to giving him orders.

The big red pickup roared out of the ranch yard. It screeched to a stop at the gate. Temo leaped out to open it, the truck gunned through and he had to run to climb aboard before Dayna sped off.

She hadn't stopped to shut the gate so Sophie ran to close it, feeling a tide of anger surge through her.

Liv could have handled Dayna! Sophie thought as she banged the gate shut and latched it. Liv would have known just what to say to that girl. Why do I feel like only half a person when Liv's not around?

## CHAPTER 9

# Horses at Wild Horse Creek

Liv urged Cactus Jack up the side of a ridge behind Shane and Navajo. She felt totally happy as she took in the wide sweep of the desert, the distant mountains, the amazingly blue sky above them.

She didn't have to worry if she was riding too fast, leaving Sophie behind, or if her sister was too hot or too tired or too anything else. How can we be so different? she wondered. We're twins. We've slept in the same room, played with the same toys, worn the same clothes, been in the same class at school all our lives! But she hates everything about this place and I'd like to live right here on this ranch, forever.

Forget her! she told herself. This was a chance to ride free and enjoy the desert without Sophie's little black cloud hanging over her. She'd get Shane to loosen up, Liv vowed, get him to explain every detail about the lizards and the cacti and all the plants beside the trail. She was sure he knew it all.

She tried to copy the way Shane rode. His lean body sat lightly on Navajo's big western saddle, perfectly balanced. His hands and shoulders and whole body moved in easy rhythm with his horse.

They rode through a low pass into Wild Horse Creek Canyon. Its steep walls rose like towers of red sandstone on either side.

A coyote, skinny and gray, dashed across their path and disappeared in the tangle of mesquite trees. Liv grinned to herself, thinking how the horse she rode back home in Vancouver would have spooked at a coyote. For Cactus Jack and Navajo, it was just an everyday event.

"Why don't I see any cows?" she hollered up to Shane. "I thought this was a cattle ranch."

"Used to be hundreds." Shane turned Navajo back to ride beside her. "But your grandparents are gettin' too old to run any cattle."

Liv said, "I guess they are — but isn't it a shame to have all this land and not use it for raising cows?"

"That's what the other ranchers around here think," Shane said. "Especially since your grandparents have the best water hole for miles around. Folks would love to get their hands on that spring."

"The water hole where we found Diego? If that's the best water hole, the rest of this land must be really dry."

Shane nodded. "That's why I think we'll find Diego's mares and foals near it. They'll have to drink."

Slowing to a walk, they followed the bed of Wild Horse Creek. It was filled with rounded stones.

"Is there ever water in this creek?" Liv frowned as she studied the dry stones.

"After the rains," Shane told her. "Usually in July ... sometimes in the fall or spring, like now."

"In Vancouver, where I come from, it rains all winter. You don't know how good it is to see the sun."

Shane smiled. "Sun pretty much every day here."

Liv saw how he peered into every clump of trees, looking for the missing horses. "Do you think they're hiding in there?"

"Not hidin'." Shane shook his head. "But they brush up in the trees, to get the shade and to keep the flies off. Can be hard to spot 'em."

Liv nodded. She was excited to see this herd she'd heard so much about. Descendents of the horses the Spanish explorers brought to Mexico five hundred years ago. Horses from Spain and North Africa, adapted to this harsh country. There used to be thousands and thousands of them running free in the West. Now only pockets were left, like her grandparents' herd.

The Starr-Lopez horses lived almost as free as their wild horse ancestors. They were tamed when they were needed for work, like Cactus Jack and Cisco, and then let go again once their working days were over so they could roam the ranch lands.

Liv stopped dreaming with a jolt. They had reached the water hole.

There they were — a small group of horses drinking near the same spot where Diego had lain, wounded.

Shane held up his hand.

Liv glanced at his face. "What's wrong?"

"This isn't Diego's herd."

"What do you mean?" gasped Liv.

"Look at their brand." Shane jammed down his hat. "Two S's. These are Silver Spur horses!" He let out a grunt. "What the blazes are they doin' here?"

Liv had no idea what he was talking about, but she could see the red flush of anger creeping up Shane's neck. Something was seriously wrong.

"These horses belong to Sam Regis, a rancher who wants this water hole," he muttered. "I don't think they're here by accident."

"But how ...?" Liv began.

"Get off your horse," Shane ordered in a low voice, "and stay back toward the trees. See there?"

As she slid from the saddle, she looked where Shane

pointed. Another small band of horses, mares with foals running beside them, came out of the trees on the opposite side of the water hole.

"*That's* the Starr-Lopez herd," Shane whispered, "and there's the lead mare, Carmelita." He nodded at a lovely sorrel mare with a white face and markings on her sides.

Beside her ran a colt that was a tiny version of Diego, with a black bottlebrush tail and four long spindly legs. "Diego's his dad?" Liv whispered, feeling tears prickle behind her eyes, the colt was so beautiful.

"You bet." Shane said.

They watched the new group mingle with the Silver Spur horses around the water hole. There was the usual jockeying for position, swinging heads and high kicks, until everybody got sorted out to drink peacefully.

A minute later they heard a high whinny of command and a black horse burst from the trees. He took in the group of grazing mares and foals like a proud owner looking over his estate.

"Who is that?" Liv said breathlessly. She had never seen such power and grace in a horse. His neck was high and arched and he carried his plumed tail like a banner.

"I – I don't know," stammered Shane. "It's a stallion, but I've never seen him before."

"Do you think this is the stallion that attacked Diego?"

"Maybe. He's got some fresh battle scars on his neck and shoulder. But what a horse! Look at that white blaze on his face and his four white socks."

Liv glanced at Shane's face. She saw a look that reminded her of her brother Mark when he was looking at a hot new racecar. Awe. Joy. Longing. All mixed in the gaze he fixed on the black stallion.

"Watch!" he whispered. "He's going to round up the new mares."

The black stallion thundered toward the horses at the water hole. Whirling and stamping, his neck outstretched, he gathered them into a tight group.

Soon it was hard to sort the Silver Spur horses from the others. They headed away from the spring, lost in a cloud of dust.

"Where is he taking them?" Liv gasped.

"That's what we have to find out." Shane swung into Navajo's saddle. "C'mon, we can't lose sight of them."

Liv grabbed Cactus Jack's saddle horn and struggled onto his back just before he broke into a jog following Navajo.

# CHAPTER 10
# Sophie is Spooked

Sophie sat on a bale of straw, hugging her knees. It was almost noon she realized, glancing at her watch. An hour had gone by since Dayna and Temo drove away and still no vet.

The barn was silent except for the stallion's restless stamping and Tux's panting. It was getting hot inside the steel-roofed building.

Tux lay in one corner of the stall. When Sophie peered over the door, he raised one eyebrow at her. He had a black patch around one eye, which made him look like a pirate.

"How's he doing, Doctor Dog?" Sophie murmured.

Diego still hadn't eaten and had only drank a small amount from his water pail.

"You stay here and keep watch," Sophie told the dog. "I'm going to see if there's a message from the vet."

The blazing noon sun hit like a stun gun as she stepped outside the barn door. She shuffled across the dusty ranch yard. The hollow eyes of the cattle skulls seemed to glare at her from the veranda. Sophie opened the screen door and stepped inside. *It's cooler in here*, she thought. The message light on the desk phone flashed red in the dim light. Sophie picked up the phone and punched in the correct code. *Lopez*, her grandmother's name.

The message was not from the vet. It was from her mother.

"I'm going to be longer than I thought," Sophie heard her mother's voice hesitate for a moment, then a noise as if her mother was blowing her nose. "Probably after dinner before I get back." There was a pause and then her mother said with forced cheerfulness, "Hope the vet had good news about Diego."

Good news? No news from the vet. Fear fluttered in Sophie's stomach. She sank down on the cowhide sofa with her head in her hands. Why had Mom sounded so weird — it wasn't her normal voice at all. Why did she have to wait in Tucson? Was Gran all right?

A loud crash and frantic neighing from the direction of the barn brought her to her feet. She banged through the screen door back to the barn.

Diego was in a fury. The horse that just a few minutes ago had seemed restless was now trying to kick down the stall walls. He lashed out with his powerful hooves pounding fiercely against the wood planks. His frantic kicks had raised a haze of dust in the barn.

Tux had somehow scrambled over the stall door and out of the way of those slashing hooves.

"What's the matter?" Sophie choked on the dust. It was as if Diego had lost his mind. What had upset him?

"Diego, calm down, you're all right." Sophie tried to sooth him but her voice shook. The stallion suddenly wheeled and lunged at the stall door, sending a bolt of terror through her body. Diego's eyes blazed fire and his nostrils flared as he stared her down. Sophie stepped back with a gasp, her heart pounding in her chest. She wanted to run.

*Liv — help!* her mind shouted, but Liv was not there. Her sister, her mother, Granddad, Shane — no one was there! No one on this whole ranch could help Diego or tell her what to do. She had never felt so alone. I can't stay here, she thought, her breath coming in frantic gasps. I have to get help.

She grabbed a saddle, a saddle blanket and a bridle off the rack in the barn. "Come on," she yelled at Tux over the thunder of Diego's frenzy. "You have to find Shane." Dragging the heavy tack, Sophie stumbled to the corral with Tux at her heels.

Cisco was drinking from the water trough. "Good

boy!" She threw the saddle blanket over Cisco's strong back and speedily saddled and bridled him. Minutes later she was closing the ranch gate behind her.

"Find Shane!" She flung herself on Cisco's back. "Tux! Go find Shane!"

Tux nosed the sand outside the gate, ran in circles, sniffing, then gave a short sharp bark and trotted ahead, tail wagging.

Sophie followed. Was this the trail to Wild Horse Creek? It was hard to tell when everything on this dry dusty desert looked the same. Dry! Sophie suddenly realized she hadn't brought a canteen. No water — but she didn't dare go back for it now. In front of her Tux was heading at top speed across the desert to find Shane. Back at the barn there was only the fury of that poor horse. Sophie could feel the panic rising again in her chest. She nudged Cisco forward and followed Tux.

❋ ❋ ❋ ❋ ❋

An hour later, thorny bushes closed in on Sophie from all sides. Did Tux know where he was going? Could this be the way Shane and Liv had traveled?

Sophie was thirstier than she'd ever been in her life. "I'm glad we fed and watered you this morning," she said to Cisco, her voice hoarse. "You can last out here in the desert — you're a Spanish horse." She bent forward to pull a thorn branch from Cisco's mane.

"Gran said horses in your line can handle heat, dry air, any kind of rough ground. Hey, hold it! Not so fast!"

Cisco had broken into a jog to keep up with Tux. The dog had dashed into a thicket of dead mesquite ahead of them.

Instinctively, Sophie leaned to one side to avoid being brushed off under one of the trees. To her horror, the saddle slid sideways with her. She grabbed for Cisco's mane, lost her balance and fell awkwardly into a heap of brush. Cisco jogged away with the saddle flopping under his belly.

Dizzy from her fall, Sophie struggled to catch her breath and sit up. She was bruised and sore but nothing seemed to be broken. Cisco was already out of sight.

"Stupid!" she blasted herself. "I forgot to check the cinch before I got on." Cisco must have taken a big deep breath when he was saddled to keep the cinch loose. Sophie knew it was routine to tighten the latigo strap a couple of holes before you mounted, but she had forgotten to do it in her panic.

Cisco could get badly hurt with the saddle hanging under him and his reins dangling free. He could trip on the reins, or get the saddle caught on a rock or a bush.

Sophie squirmed out of the tangle of mesquite and edged past a prickly pear cactus studded with long horrible thorns. What if she'd landed on that!

"Tux!" she called. "Where are you?"

But there was no sign of the border collie. He had his orders to find Shane and was probably far away by now.

And where was she? Sophie wondered. Even if they

had started out on the trail to Wild Horse Creek Canyon, Tux had cut across country not far from the ranch. She stared at her watch. That had been more than an hour ago.

She climbed a steep, stony ridge, watching for rattlesnakes, hoping she'd see the entrance to Wild Horse Creek Canyon when she reached the top. Instead she looked over a flat sweep of desert stretching away to a range of distant mountains. Wisps of gray clouds were gathering over the jagged mountain peaks.

Sophie saw nothing she recognized. No ranches, no houses or buildings, no roads, not even telephone poles. Only dead-looking brush and dry red sand as far as she could see.

# CHAPTER 11
# Lost!

Sophie turned her back on the empty desert and sank down on a rock. I'm lost, she thought. I'm going to die of thirst and turn into bleached white bones like those cattle skulls on the veranda. Swallowing was agony. Why hadn't she gone back for water?

She scrambled down to the shelter of some high rocks leaning against each other like kids' blocks. She tried to remember what she had read and seen on TV about desert survival. Don't try to walk — you might get more lost. Don't waste effort moving — it will just make you thirstier. Stay out of the sun. But if she stayed here under the shade of these rocks, how would anybody find her?

Sophie put her head down on her knees and squeezed her eyes shut to keep from crying. She must not waste water. Not even a tear.

All at once, she was aware of something else besides her overpowering thirst — a horrible smell that was getting stronger by the second. She wrinkled her nose in disgust. For someone used to the fragrance of green moss on cedar trees, damp wind and the ocean, she'd experienced lots of new desert smells in the past few days. Sharp, spicy, pungent smells. But this was different! Worse than wet dogs, and almost as bad as skunk.

She heard a strange clacking noise and opened her eyes.

A collection of weird animals trotted toward her. They were the size of large dogs, but with skinny legs and hoofs. Their heads were enormous, their eyes small and their bottom teeth stuck out like tusks. They looked like hairy pigs with white collars, and the clicking noise seemed to be coming from their jaws.

And the smell!

Sophie clapped her hand to her nose and stood up.

The animals stopped. The clacking grew louder. The lead animal spread its jaws wide and Sophie could see that its two bottom teeth curved to sharp-looking points.

"Go away!" she shouted, lunging at them.

The lead animal growled, others answered, and the whole herd rushed to attack. Sophie turned and stumbled down the ridge with the growling, clacking animals close behind. They were gaining on her! In her panic, she tripped over a rock in her path and fell full-length on the stony ground, bashing her cheek.

A tide of stink washed over Sophie. She heard the scrabble of sharp hoofs on either side. She threw her arms over her head for protection and felt a sharp blow on her left elbow as the animals swept over, around and past her.

The sound and the horrible smell faded. She sat up, spitting sand and holding her throbbing elbow. Her cheek burned where it had hit the dirt. When she tried to stand, her right ankle buckled painfully. It was the same leg the rattlesnake had bit.

"More bad luck!" Sophie groaned to herself. She limped back to the shelter of the rocks.

What on earth had those creatures been? Maybe I'm hallucinating, she thought. They say people who are dying of thirst see visions. Visions of lakes, she realized, not of hairy pigs thundering over you!

She crawled back under the tall leaning rocks. The sun beat down and black circling birds appeared high in the dazzling blue sky. Vultures! Already gathering.

"Tux!" Sophie screamed. "Tux, Shane, Liv, anybody! Here I am!"

There was no answer — nothing but the hot silence of the desert. Fear gripped Sophie's stomach and a part of her brain shrieked — *this is what happens when you and*

*Liv get separated! You're crazy if you think you can get along without your twin sister.*

*✻ ✻ ✻ ✻ ✻*

Liv and Shane followed the band of horses deeper and deeper into Wild Horse Creek Canyon. Shane rode slowly, not pushing the stallion and his mares, just staying within sight and earshot. When they stopped, he and Liv stopped too. They could see the black stallion on a high point of rock, like an eagle perched on a high branch.

"Have a drink while we're takin' a break," Shane reminded Liv.

She twisted in the saddle and unfastened her saddlebag. The canteen was cold and heavy in her hand. As she raised it to her lips, Liv felt faint. Her stomach grew as cold as the canteen.

"What's the matter?" She heard Shane's voice through a gray haze in front of her eyes.

"I — don't know." Liv lowered the canteen. "I have the most awful feeling. I can't drink this." She screwed the lid back on the green canteen. "I feel as if something's wrong — with the water, or — I know this sounds crazy — but with Sophie."

"She's back at the ranch. She's okay," Shane said. He rode closer to peer at her face.

"I know, but —"

"You'd better take that drink. You look pale."

Liv undid the cap again and held the canteen to her

lips. She felt the cool water trickle down her throat. Suddenly she choked. Coughing violently, she handed the canteen to Shane. "Here! I can't. Shane, I'm really scared. What if something has happened to Sophie?"

"Have you ever felt this before?" Shane gave her an odd look from under the brim of his hat. "Like something's the matter with your twin?"

"A few times." Liv nodded. "Usually it's something stupid, like she's forgotten her French book." She gulped. "I was so glad Sophie wasn't with us, slowing us down, complaining about everything. But I shouldn't have left her."

"I'm sure she's all right." Shane shrugged.

"You think so?"

"I don't believe in mental telepathy." Shane pointed to where the mares and foals had started off through a grove of trees. "Look, those horses are on the move again. We'd better get goin'."

Liv stuffed the canteen back in her saddlebag, but the scared feeling hadn't gone away. She followed Shane and Navajo on Cactus Jack, letting her horse do all the work, trying to sort out the muddle in her head.

Wild Horse Creek Canyon narrowed to a thin strip of rocky ground on either side of the creek. The red towers of rock pressed in on them like a vise. In some places, enormous boulders were piled on top of slender pillars. They looked as though they could come tumbling down at any second.

"Where will the horses go now?" Liv called to Shane.

"There's a fork in the creek," he called back. "Leads into Bobcat Canyon. He might be taking them in there."

Hoofs clattered over tumbled rock as their horses crossed the dry creek and took the left fork into the second canyon. Liv was amazed at how Shane knew exactly where they were headed. She felt very far from the ranch and Sophie.

Around a bend, the fork of the creek opened into a wider canyon.

They heard the black stallion whinny a command and the group of mares and foals ahead of them streamed up the side of the streambed and into a cluster of live oak and pinion pines.

"Something's spooked them," cried Shane, urging Navajo forward. Liv didn't need to nudge Cactus Jack with her legs. He took off after Shane's horse as though he'd gotten a green light.

The band streaked out of sight up the pine-covered slope. Riding down the opposite slope on the other side of the creek, Sophie saw a pair of riders on matching palominos — beautiful pale gold horses with paler manes and streaming tails.

The riders rode straight toward Shane and pulled up in a cloud of dust.

"Were those our horses you were chasing?" The man on the first palomino had a red face under his white hat. He wore fancy riding clothes and expensive-looking boots. The girl on the golden horse behind him had a ponytail to match her horse. She pulled up beside Shane.

"Hey, Shane," she said. "I was looking for you."

"Hey, Dayna," he answered mildly. "We weren't runnin' your horses. What were they doin' drinkin' at Starr's water hole?"

"How is that your business," the red-faced rider spluttered.

"Stop shouting, Daddy. He works for Mr. Starr. Don't you, Shane?" the girl said. "Shouldn't we find out what's happened to our horses?"

"Isn't it obvious? We caught these two chasing them up Bobcat Canyon!" He seemed to notice Liv for the first time. "Who's that?"

"I don't know," Dayna Regis shrugged. "But she looks like the kid Temo and I saw at the Starr ranch today."

"You saw Sophie?" Liv shot in. "She's my twin sister. Is she okay?"

"Looked fine," the girl drawled. "Just a little pasty, if you know what I mean."

"Liv, this is Sam Regis and his daughter Dayna," Shane growled. "They own those horses we saw at the spring."

# CHAPTER 12
# A Pair of Palominos

Liv had a hard time taking her eyes off the two palominos. They were exquisitely built and beautifully colored — a perfect match. She glanced at Sam Regis. So this was the man her granddad had accused of wounding Diego — the guy who wanted to get hold of his land, and his water.

"Your horses have joined up with the Starr herd," Shane told him quietly. "They ran off together — maybe because they haven't got Diego to lead them. I expect they'll come back to the spring if we quit chasin' them." He tipped his hat to the older man. "I'll see that your bunch get back to your spread."

Why didn't Shane tell Sam Regis about the black stallion? Liv wondered.

"I heard Diego had an accident," Sam said. "Too bad." There was a sneer in his voice.

"He looks terrible," Dayna added.

They're not sorry. They're glad Diego's hurt, Liv realized with a jolt of anger. They're a pair of big fakers!

She was about to open her mouth to protest when Shane wheeled Navajo around and cut her off. "We'll get goin'," he said. "Come on, Liv."

He led the way down the canyon. As soon as the palominos were out of sight, he stopped. "Good place to have a drink and eat those sandwiches you fixed," he said, slipping from Navajo's saddle.

Liv pulled Cactus Jack to a halt, jumped from the saddle and pulled the package of sandwiches from her saddle bag. "Why didn't you tell Mr. Regis about the black stallion rounding up his horses?" she asked.

Shane took a long drink from his canteen. "Because he's the kind of guy who would go home and get his high-powered rifle and shoot that stallion," he said, and Liv could hear the quiet fury behind his words. "He thinks every wild horse is a *mestengo* — a no-good rogue horse that should be destroyed before he can corrupt his purebred herd."

"Oh," Liv said, "is that why he hates Diego?" She handed Shane a sandwich.

"Partly," Shane told her. "But he also knows that

without Diego, the Starr-Lopez horses would be easy to disperse and he'd have a better chance of getting hold of your grandparents' ranch."

Liv stared at him. "It looks so beautiful and peaceful here in the desert. As though bad things could never happen."

Shane gave a short laugh. "Not true," he said. "This is a blood-soaked stretch of land. There were wars with Spain and then wars with Mexico, wars against the Indians, wars between rival tribes — lots of fightin' and hatin' and killin'." He looked up at the canyon walls. "Right here used to be a stronghold for the Apaches, where they could fight off the Rangers who were tryin' to round them up."

"That was a long time ago," Liv reminded him.

"Sure, but now we have border guards chasin' Mexicans who try to cross the border illegally. And we got poachers after the wild horses and all kinds of other bad stuff goin' on." Shane shook his head and took a bite of his sandwich.

"Like Mr. Regis, letting his horses stray onto Granddad's land? Did he do that on purpose?" Liv asked angrily.

"Might have." Shane made a motion with his hand. "But he's gone now. Time for us to be after that black stallion and his bunch. Better have something to eat."

"I can't eat," Liv said. "Shane, I know finding the horses is important, but first I want to go back to the ranch and make sure Sophie's all right. Remember how I felt when I tried to take a drink? That feeling's still here." She made a fist in the middle of her belly. "It won't go away."

"You don't really believe in that premonition stuff, do you?" Shane tipped his hat back and gazed at her.

"I — I don't know. But whether I believe it or not I have to make sure."

"We might never catch that stallion if we don't go now," Shane said, yanking his hat down on his forehead. "He could be headed for Mexico."

"Then you go and chase him. I'm going back." Liv put her sandwich in the saddle bag and swung into Cactus Jack's saddle.

"Wait a minute. I can't let you do that!" Shane burst out. "You could get lost trying to find your way to the ranch."

"I don't think so," Liv picked up Cactus Jack's reins. "It's just down this canyon to the fork and then follow Wild Horse Creek to the spring and then —" She stopped, uncertain of the route.

Shane was still shaking his head. His neck was turning red. "Can't let you do it," he repeated. "If you're that stubborn, I'll have to come with you."

"I'm not stubborn!" Liv flared up. "I'm scared. I'm really scared that something's happened to Sophie!"

Shane didn't say anything. He just mounted Navajo, clucked to his horse and headed back the way they'd come. *He's disgusted with me*, Liv thought. *He thinks I'm stubborn and ridiculous*.

It felt strange to be the one holding back, being careful. Normally she'd be in the lead racing after that band of horses. If only she didn't have this nagging sick feeling. She'd been wrong to leave Sophie alone with Diego. She'd been selfish, wanting to ride across the desert with Shane, wanting freedom.

They rode through Bobcat Canyon to the fork into Wild Horse Creek Canyon. As they rounded a bend, they heard a familiar yelp and Tux came racing toward them. He circled Navajo, barking joyfully.

Shane slid from his saddle in one smooth move. "Tux!" He caught the dog in his arms. "What are you doing here? I left you in charge of Diego."

Liv felt her stomach sink. "Oh, Shane," she gulped. "Tux wouldn't have left Sophie and Diego if everything was all right, would he?"

Shane shrugged, still ruffling Tux's shaggy coat. "He came to find me. Mebbe Sophie sent him."

"Because she's in trouble!" Liv cried, trying to swallow. She tried to think what Sophie would do. But her mind was a blank. There was just this sick feeling.

"Look!" she pointed. The dog had wriggled out of Shane's arms and raced back the way he had come. "Tux wants us to follow him."

Shane shoved his hat down tight. "Looks like you're right," he mumbled. He mounted up and they rode after Tux, who kept dashing ahead, and then running back to make sure they were coming.

Liv wanted to ride faster, but the trail was too stony for a lope in most places. Cactus Jack seemed to sense her worry and broke into a brisk jog down each slope. Dust rose around them as they rode through the pass at the canyon's end out into the dry chaparral.

All at once, Tux hurtled off to the left, heading into the thick tangle of trees and bushes.

"Hey, Tux, buddy, where are you headin'?" Shane called. "That's not the way to the ranch. Come here, boy."

But the dog paid no attention. He was soon out of sight and all they could hear was his eager yelps.

"Shouldn't we follow him?" Liv rode Cactus Jack up beside Shane. "Maybe Sophie is somewhere over there."

"In that mess of brush?" Shane shoved back his hat and wiped his forehead. "There's nothin' but cactus and thorny wait-a-minute bushes that catch at your clothes. Tough ridin'. I should know. I've had to chase cows that are brushed up in that stuff. Can't even spot 'em till you're right on top of them. Why would Sophie go that way?"

He urged Navajo forward on the wide trail to the ranch.

"Wait! Sophie might be lost. We should stay with Tux." Liv pushed her own hat down harder. If Sophie was in that wild chaparral, she'd be hard to spot, too.

Tux was still yapping off in the distance.

"We should look." Liv shouted. "Please Shane!"

"You are the craziest girl I ever met," Shane muttered.

But he swung his reins over Navajo's neck and the buckskin paint turned obediently into the brush.

"Keep your head down," he shouted, "or you're liable to get a thorn branch in your face."

Liv yanked down her hat and leaned forward, hugging herself as close to Cactus Jack's body as she could. Her horse almost ran into Navajo. Shane had stopped in a dense ticket of red-barked manzanita bushes.

"This is as far as we go," he muttered. "Smell that wicked stink? There's a herd of javelinas around here somewhere."

"Hava-whats?" The pungent, skunky smell made Liv wrinkle her nose.

"Javelinas," Shane said. "Critters that smell bad and look like pigs — but they're actually peccaries with two big tusks as sharp as knives."

"Are they dangerous?"

"Not unless you bother 'em," Shane said. "That's why we're gettin' out of here. We don't want thirty or forty javelinas charging us in this thick brush."

"But look!" Liv pointed. Vultures were circling some high rocks in the distance. The sick feeling in Liv's stomach rose to her throat. "It could be Sophie!"

# CHAPTER 13
# Vultures!

Shane squinted at the circling birds. "When you live in the desert," he told Liv, "you get used to seeing vultures. We'd better move along. Those javelinas could be anywhere in this brush."

Liv turned back reluctantly. The feeling that they should go on to those tall rocks was so strong.

Just then they heard a rustling and a stomping in the brush to their right.

"Javelinas?" Liv cried. They heard a frantic whinny.

"No sir!" Shane jumped from his saddle. "That's a horse!" He dived through a screen of mesquite. "Jumpin' jackrabbits," he called. "It's Cisco!"

"Sophie! Are you there?" Liv scrambled after him.

"No," she heard Shane shout. "Your sister's not here and her horse is a mess."

On the other side of the spreading bush, Liv found Shane struggling to heave Cisco's saddle back in place and retrieve his dangling reins. "Shane," she gulped. "What's happened to Sophie?"

"Looks like her saddle slipped sideways and she fell off." He freed Cisco from the tangle of thorns, tightened his cinch and led him through the thick brush to the other horses.

"She can't be too far," he muttered with a worried frown. "We'd better climb that ridge where you saw the buzzards circlin'. Beyond that ridge is a big dry lake. If Sophie's out there, she's in real trouble. Come on!"

He mounted Navajo with Cisco's reins in his hand and pushed ahead.

They rode through the chaparral, heads up, searching every gully and wash for a sign of Sophie. "Looks as though Cisco's been wandering back and forth." Shane pointed to his hoof prints in the deep sand of a dry wash.

There was no sign of Sophie's footprints.

They were climbing steadily upward. Liv kept her eye on the birds. As they rode closer to the tall rocks, she could see their bald red heads drooping between enormous black wings as they soared over the desert, round and round.

Then they heard Tux. It was his high, commanding bark, not a friendly woof or his cheerful yapping. And it was coming from the direction of the rocks.

"She must be up there!" Liv didn't know whether to be reassured or even more frightened.

✳ ✳ ✳ ✳ ✳

Sophie lay with her eyes squeezed shut, trying to block out the sun, the burning pain in her ankle and the killing thirst.

She thought she heard a dog bark. Was she dreaming? She opened her eyes to see Tux's black and white body streaking toward her. He threw himself at her face, licking her parched cheeks.

"Tux!" She could barely croak his name. "Is that really you, boy?" She wrapped her arms around him. It was Tux all right, warm and wiggly and panting for joy to have found her.

"Where's Liv and Shane?" she tried to ask, but the words came out in a hoarse squeak.

Tux wriggled out of her arms and stood barking at the vultures, which lifted slowly into the sky.

All of a sudden, the dog dashed away.

"Tux, don't go! Please don't leave me!" Sophie begged. "Oh, please come back."

But he was gone, and the desert silence settled on her once again. A feeling of hopelessness washed over her. Without Tux, the birds would come for her. They'd claw at her eyes ...

And then she heard shouting. "So — phie! Where are you?"

She sat up. Tried to stand but couldn't. "I'm ... here," she croaked, her throat like sandpaper. "I'm here!"

Minutes later, Tux was in her arms again and behind him, shimmering in the heat waves, were Shane on Navajo and Liv on Cactus Jack. Were they a mirage?

No, it was Liv! She was leaping off her horse, hugging her so tight Sophie thought she would suffocate.

"Sophie!" Liv sobbed. "I knew you were in trouble."

"I'm glad you came," Sophie whispered. "Have you got ... any water?"

Shane was already handing her an open canteen. "Just a little bit," he warned. "You'll throw up if you drink too fast."

Sophie tipped up the canteen with a shaking hand. Liv helped her hold it steady. Cool water filled her mouth and throat. She spluttered and coughed.

"Okay. Okay. I'll be all right, now." She reached out to pat Tux, who sat, panting into her face.

"He's a good cow dog." Shane grinned down at them. "Always finds the strays."

Liv was staring at Sophie's bruised cheek. "What happened to your face?"

Sophie gulped. "A herd of animals that looked like hairy pigs attacked me. I fell and twisted my ankle and scraped my face on the ground. Ugh! You should have smelled them!"

"We did smell them. Horrible! They're called javelinas."

"Those critters can be dangerous," Shane said, once more removing her boot. "You're lucky you didn't get hurt worse." He felt her ankle. "It's a bit swollen. Sophie — what in blazes were you doin' out here by yourself with no water?"

Sophie took a deep breath to try to explain. "Diego was going crazy. I didn't know what to do and I was afraid he was going to hurt himself, kicking at the stall like that. The vet didn't come ..." She knew her explanation sounded weak and stupid.

"Don't worry," Shane stuffed Sophie's boot in his saddle bag. "That stall Diego's in is strong — likely the safest place for him."

"I should have known that." Sophie swallowed hard. "I guess I panicked — being by myself. Mom left a message that she was going to be late. I — I thought I'd better find you." She looked up at Liv. "Mom sounded funny — as if something was wrong. So I ... I told Tux to look for you, and this is where he led me."

"Tux!" Shane grabbed his dog by the scruff of his neck and gave him an affectionate shake. "What were you thinkin' leading Cisco and Sophie off the trail into this thorn brush?"

Tux gave a doggy grin.

"Did you find Diego's herd?" Sophie asked.

"A gorgeous black stallion with a white blaze rounded them up with some horses from Silver Spur Ranch," Liv explained breathlessly. "Shane thinks he might be a wild horse. He wanted to go after them, but —"

"Your sister, here, insisted that we find you first." Shane finished her sentence. "Claimed she knew you were in trouble. Good thing for you she did."

"We'll stick together from now on," Liv promised. She linked her forefinger with Sophie's and smiled.

Their old signal! Sophie gulped. When they were little, even before they could talk, they'd had that secret sign, but Liv hadn't done it in ages.

"Stick together." Sophie nodded, brushing away tears. She was crying with relief, but part of her cried for that moment when she'd wanted to move into Gran's room, ready to fight for a little space of her own.

"We should get you back on your horse," Shane said gently. "Can you walk?"

"If you help."

Sophie felt Shane's strong arms lift her up, and with him on one side and Liv on the other she limped to Cisco.

"I was an idiot not to check your cinch," she murmured, laying her head against the horse's copper-colored cheek. "I hope you're not hurt."

"Just a little scratched up," Shane said. "Like you." He shook his head as he heaved Sophie into the saddle. "I can't believe you came out here with no water."

# CHAPTER 14
# Temo's News

"Have another drink." Shane handed the canteen up to Sophie. "Then we should get you back to the ranch."

"What about the horses?" Sophie swallowed the water gratefully. "And the black stallion?"

"Probably halfway to Mexico by now." Shane leaped onto Navajo's saddle. "Unless they circled back to the water hole."

Sophie could feel his disappointment at his lost chance to capture Diego's mares. If it hadn't been for me, he would have found them, she thought. It's the second time I've messed up looking for Diego's herd — if only I hadn't got so scared, being on my own.

She guided Cisco into line behind Navajo with Liv bringing up the rear. They zigzagged their way through the thick brush.

As they came out on the main trail to the ranch, a rider on a black and white paint horse flew toward them from the direction of the Lucky Star Ranch.

"*Hola*! Shane!" The rider drew up beside Shane in a rising cloud of dust.

"Temo!" Shane exclaimed. "What's up, buddy?"

"I was looking for you at the ranch, *amigo*. The vet was there checking on Diego. The stallion was pretty riled up. Something must have spooked him. Maybe he smelled a bobcat or a coyote —"

Sophie broke in. "Is Diego okay? I knew I shouldn't have left him alone."

Temo smiled at Sophie from under the brim of his black hat. "I wondered where you'd gone," he called over to her " — thought you might be inside having a *siesta*. Anyway, the vet calmed Diego down. He's fine. Put a couple of stitches in his shoulder. The *manadero* will be good as new."

Sophie heard Liv's quick intake of breath as she pulled Cactus Jack level with Cisco. "Wow!" she whispered. "Have you ever seen a more gorgeous guy? I wonder who he is." Sophie gave Liv a quick glance. Two spots of color glowed in her sister's cheeks and her eyes danced.

"Listen!" Sophie hissed. "He's got some news about Diego's mares."

"Someone called my boss, Señor Regis," Temo was saying. "A small plane, flying low, spotted some horses heading south, led by a *mestengo* — a black stallion."

"We saw them." Shane pushed back his hat. "Out in Bobcat Canyon. What's Regis going to do? He can't be too happy about a stray mustang making off with his mares."

Temo frowned. "He's going after them, taking all the *vaqueros* from the ranch to round up the band and destroy the *mestengo*." He paused. "I thought you should know. Most of the mares and foals belong to this ranch, not to Regis."

"Is Señor Regis the same guy that we met?" asked Liv, urging her horse closer to Temo. "The one with the blonde daughter and the matching palominos?"

Temo nodded. "*Sí*, yes. That would be Señor Regis, and his daughter Dayna." He whipped off his broad black hat. "*Hola*, Señorita," he said politely. "You must be Sophie's sister."

"We're twins," Liv said. She gave Sophie an astonished glance "You ... know him?"

"My name is Temo Diaz," Temo said. He looked straight into Liv's eyes and smiled.

Sophie could see her sister's hand quiver as she reached out to shake Temo's hand. "Pleased to ... meet you," Liv murmured.

"I'm happy to meet Señor and Señora Starr's granddaughters." Temo was still holding Liv's hand. Now

101

he let it go. "I have get back to the Silver Spur Ranch," he told them. "I'll be riding with Señor Regis and his men, but I will do what I can to help your grandparents' horses. *Adiós, muchachas*."

He jammed his hat back on and took off down the sandy track at a gallop.

When he'd gone, Liv reached over to tug Shane's sleeve. "*Adiós* — that's Spanish for goodbye. What does *muchachas* mean?"

Shane shrugged. "It means kids. 'So long, kids', is what he said."

"Oh." Liv looked disappointed. "And he works for that father-and-daughter team we met — the ones with the beautiful palominos?"

Shane nodded.

"You didn't mention meeting Mr. Regis and his daughter," said Sophie.

"Well, you didn't mention meeting Temo!" Liv shot back. "Is he from Mexico?"

"His family comes from Mexico and he's lived there on and off, but Temo was born in Arizona," Shane explained.

"He came to the ranch with Dayna, looking for Shane," Sophie told her.

"Well, he was nice to come back and warn us about Mr. Regis's plans." Liv stared after him. "What are we going to do, Shane?"

Shane said slowly, "I'd sure like to try to stop Regis

rounding up Diego's mares, but that would mean a lot of hard ridin'. I don't think Sophie's up to it, after what she's been through. We'd better head for the ranch."

There was a long pause. Tux whined as if he knew there was an important decision to be made.

"I'm up to it." Sophie said at last, with another glance at Liv's flushed face. She knew Liv was dying to go after Diego's herd and the mystery stallion, and maybe even meet up with Temo again.

"I don't know." Shane shook his head.

"Come on, Shane," Sophie urged. "Granddad would want us to go after his horses — and I'll keep up. I promise not to fall off my horse or forget to drink."

A smile spread across Shane's lean face. "Okay, if you're sure."

"Thank you, Sophie!" Liv reached over and squeezed her arm. "Where do you think the black stallion has taken the herd?" she asked Shane as she turned Cactus Jack and they headed toward Wild Horse Creek Canyon and Wild Horse Creek.

"I'm hopin' he's circled round and brought the bunch back to the water hole." Shane urged Navajo forward. "If not, he might be anywhere between here and the Mexican border. I'll ride first so I can track the horses."

"How far is the border?" Sophie called to him.

"Only about twenty miles as the crow flies," Shane called back, 'But there's mighty rough country between here and there. Hope we don't have to cross it."

"Me, too!" Liv said quickly. "No more steep mountain trails. No more adventures, right Sophie?"

They covered the trail through the low pass at a fast clip. The wind had risen, blowing dust in their faces. Shane pointed up to a heap of gray clouds rolling over the jagged peaks to the south. "We might get some rain," he shouted.

"I thought it never rained," Sophie called.

"Never enough," Shane hollered back. "But we get thunderstorms, real gully washers."

"What's a gully washer?" Liv yelled.

"You'll see, if it comes." Shane led the way into the depths of the canyon.

They followed the creek in silence till they reached the water hole. There was no sign of the black stallion or the mares and foals.

Shane studied the trampled mud. "They haven't been back here," he said. He looked up at the canyon walls. "They're either hidin' in a side canyon somewhere, or they've hightailed it south. That stallion likely knows every spring and water hole between here and Mexico."

"How will we find them?" asked Liv.

"Keep goin' and watch for tracks," Shane said. "Sophie? How are you doin'? Need a rest?"

"I'm fine. Let's go on. I'm okay, honest," Sophie said. Shane was still thinking of her as weak and helpless. She would show him! It was her fault they'd lost the trail of the Starr-Lopez horses. This time, she wouldn't give up till they found them.

# CHAPTER 15
# **Helicopter Chase**

Shane spotted the tracks half an hour later. He stepped out of Navajo's shadow to study the faint hoof prints in brighter light. Tux sniffed all around the tracks, then sat back on his haunches with his eyes fixed on Shane's face.

"It's Diego's bunch." Shane straightened up with a worried frown. "Twenty or thirty unshod mares and foals. And here —" He pointed to another faint track, " — other horses with shoes. That'll be the Silver Spur horses. And here! A horse and rider." He took off his hat and banged it against his knee. Dust rose in a cloud. "That will be one of the cowhands from the Regis ranch."

"Maybe Temo!" Liv cried. At the memory of the

young cowboy, Liv shifted in her saddle. Those eyes! Almost black they were so brown, but the way they lit up when Temo smiled at her!

"How can you tell all that?" Sophie leaned over Cisco's neck to look at the faint marks.

"I've been tracking animals since I was ten," Shane explained. "It's like readin' a book to me."

"So the Regis cowhands and Temo aren't far ahead," said Liv. "Think we can catch up?"

Shane nodded. "We can likely catch them," he said. "I'm just not sure what to do then."

"What do you mean?" Liv frowned. "They're our horses."

"Yeah, but we're just three kids against some pretty tough men, and maybe a rifle," Shane said slowly. "Not much of a chance."

"Temo will help us," Liv said.

Shane shook his head. "That *hombre* already took a big risk warning us what Regis was up to," he muttered. "He has to be careful."

"Why?" Liv stared at him. "Why does he have to be careful?"

"That's Temo's business." Shane climbed back in the saddle. "Not mine to tell."

There was some kind of mystery about him, thought Liv. She hoped she'd get to know Temo and find out all about him before she left. The thought of saying goodbye to all this made Liv groan out loud. She never wanted to leave.

They made the turn into Bobcat Canyon. Shane stopped and leaned forward, breaking off a spiny branch of catclaw acacia. "They came this way," he said. "Here's a horse hair where a horse brushed the thorns. Looks like it's from the black stallion."

"Wow — you've got good eyes." Liv threw him an admiring glance. "I never would have seen that."

"You have to know what you're looking for." Shane turned to look back at Sophie. "How's it goin'?" he asked again.

"Good. I'm fine." Sophie straightened in the saddle.

Liv turned to scan Sophie's face. She knew Sophie wouldn't complain even if every muscle in her body was screaming. But her sister's tight lips and the grip of her hands on the reins were signs that she wished she was anywhere else but in this desert canyon. Liv smoothed Cactus Jack's mane and sighed. She could read her twin's face and body language the way Shane could read the trail.

As they made their way up the canyon, the walls of red rock pressed in closer.

"It looks like a dead end," Liv called to Shane.

"We climb up there," Shane pointed to the ridge ahead of them. "The trail's not too steep."

"Did you hear that, Sophie?" Liv asked. "Not a hard climb."

She could see Sophie nod, her lips tighter than ever.

Just then a rattling roar filled the air. Above them, a

gray helicopter appeared. It hovered over the ridge for a second, and then dropped down out of sight.

Shane swore.

"What's happening?" Liv shouted over the roar of the helicopter's blades.

Shane rode back beside her. "Looks like Sam Regis might have hired a 'copter to herd the horses."

"Using a helicopter to herd horses?" Liv shouted. "Can they do that?"

"The Bureau of Land Management uses helicopters and planes to drive wild horses into traps all the time," Shane yelled back. "The horses don't have much of a chance."

The gray helicopter was hard to spot against the dark clouds that had piled up over the canyon rim.

"But can anyone hire a helicopter?" Liv shaded her eyes, trying to see it.

"Sam Regis isn't just anyone." Shane urged Navajo forward. "He's a powerful, rich guy. Come on! I want to see this."

Liv could hear the anger in Shane's voice. She gave Cactus Jack the signal to go, but he didn't need any urging to follow Navajo up the trail. Liv turned and saw Sophie struggling to keep up. "Lean forward," she called to her sister. "Give him his head." Sophie was holding Cisco's reins too tightly in her nervousness.

"I'm trying!" Sophie shouted.

The canyon ended in loose gravelly rock, which was

hard for the horses to scramble up. As Liv and Shane crested the ridge, Liv saw the land open up into a valley shaped like a shallow basin, rimmed with jagged peaks. "Oh!" she cried. The basin was breathtaking, studded with small mesas and buttes.

She had no time to take in more of the scenery. A savage drama was taking place below them.

The black stallion was circling his band, head up, tail streaming. The cowhands from the Silver Spur ranch thundered on either side, hooting and hollering and waving their hats.

From above, the helicopter swept down, buzzing the frightened horses, driving them east toward one side of the desert basin.

"He's trying to herd them toward the Silver Spur Ranch." Shane pointed to a collection of buildings just visible to their left. He swung around. "And over there are the Sierra Madre Mountains, which might be where the stallion wants to take them."

"Shane! Look at those clouds!" Liv was seeing another drama taking place in the sky. Massive thunderheads, dark gray on the bottom, billowing white on the top, loomed over the desert floor. Liv had never seen a storm coming from such a great distance. The clouds seemed to reach up forever, towering and menacing.

"Could be a storm coming." The wind whipped the words out of Shane's mouth. "But sometimes the clouds build up like that and then it all blows away." He held onto his hat with one hand. "C'mon, we've got to get down there!"

Liv turned over her shoulder to see Sophie and Cisco struggling up the last few feet of gravel. "Hurry Sophie," Liv called back to her sister. Despite her fear for Diego's horses, Liv wanted to be in the middle of the action with the cowboys and the horses, racing across the desert floor with the wild stallion and the wild clouds above her.

She followed Shane and Tux down the zigzag trail to the valley floor, with just a backward glance to make sure Sophie had made the ridge.

# CHAPTER 16
## Roundup

As she reached the crest of the ridge, Sophie took a deep breath, shut her eyes and imagined she was home in Vancouver. When she opened them again she hoped she'd see tall trees, green grass and spring flowers — yellow daffodils and red tulips everywhere.

But no such luck. When she opened her eyes, there was just more dry brown desert. It seemed to stretch off in the distance forever, lonely and empty. The helicopter swooped over her head, making Cisco snort and rear.

Shane and Liv were already riding swiftly down the slope with Tux scampering in front. She'd never keep up. If only I hadn't been such a coward! Sophie groaned to herself, I'd be back at the ranch right now. Maybe Mom's there. Poor Diego! I've messed things up so badly — I can't fall apart now — I have to keep going.

She took another deep breath and urged Cisco forward.

The wind blew against them, making progress harder. Sophie's hat blew away in a gust. The storm clouds lowered like a lid on the desert basin. Dust and mist swirled about the roundup below.

Liv, Tux and Shane were waiting for her on a knoll near the valley floor from where they could see clearly.

"What are they doing?" Sophie shouted to Shane as she rode up to them. "I can't tell what's going on."

Shane pointed through the swirling dust. "The Regis cowboys are trying to separate the stallion from the other horses —"

The main bunch, made up of Diego's mares and foals and the Silver Spur horses, swept away to the east with the cowboys riding hard.

"They've done it!" Shane yelled. "The *mestengo* is off on his own now."

"The helicopter's after him — oh! Shane, what are they going to do?" Liv grabbed at Shane's arm. "Is that a gun?"

The 'copter swooped low. Someone leaned out of the open door with a rifle.

"They're going to shoot him!" Liv screamed. "We've got to stop them!"

"We're too far away!" Shane shook his head.

The black stallion streaked across the valley floor, heading south, a vision of pure flowing motion. Nothing on earth could catch him, but the helicopter, like a large gray insect, tracked him easily.

"It's against the law to shoot him, isn't it?" Sophie gasped.

"Regis isn't worried about the law," Shane growled. He turned around on Navajo to block their view. "You'd better not watch this."

Tux growled low in his throat, as if he understood that something bad was going to happen.

Sophie squeezed her hands over her ears, waiting for the rifle crack.

But the crack that split the air was not a rifle shot. A bolt of lightning lashed above the fleeing horse and the thunderclap that followed was like a hundred cannons.

The helicopter hung in midair.

Another bolt of lightning lit the sky above the desert. The 'copter wavered. They watched in awe as it dipped and turned, heading back toward the valley wall, away from the lightning forks and the running black horse.

The stallion ran on and as the skies opened and rain fell in great sweeping sheets, he vanished from their view.

Shane took off his hat, waved it in the air and whooped for joy. "He made it!" he shouted. "Thanks to the storm — it's an almighty gully washer, for sure!"

In seconds, they were drenched.

"Come on." Shane shouted over the howling of the wind. "I've got to find you girls some shelter." He wheeled away on Navajo. "Man!" he hollered, "That's some horse. I'd sure like to see him again some day."

✳ ✳ ✳ ✳ ✳

As they reached the valley floor, Temo rode toward them out of the rain. Liv recognized his black and white paint horse and his big black hat.

"You saw?" His face was crimson with excitement. "The *mestengo* got away!"

Liv gasped. "Where are they taking Diego's herd?" she asked him. "Do you know?"

"*Sí*. That's what I came to tell you. I heard Señor Regis talking to the ranch foreman. He's putting your *remuda* in a corral at Silver Spur. What I don't like is that he has brought in an eighteen-wheeler horse transport. Maybe he's thinking of shipping the Lucky Star horses away somewhere. He could always say the *mestengo* kidnapped them —"

Temo paused for breath.

"Thanks for the warning, buddy," Shane said grimly.

"What are you going to do, *amigo*?"

"Don't know. I should get these girls out of the rain."

"*Sí*, the *muchachas* — they are getting very wet." The rain was coming down harder now, splashing red mud up the horses' legs and soaking them to the skin.

"There's a small hay barn at Silver Spur where you

115

could shelter," Temo said. "And maybe, later, you can think of a way to save your horses. I've got to go." He wheeled his horse around. "Look for a barn with a red roof behind the main corral. And try to stay out of sight," Temo warned. "Regis is going to be plenty mad about that stallion getting away."

With a whoop, he took off across the rain-swept valley.

Liv wished she could follow. It felt like something pulled at her insides, watching Temo ride away. He was so brave to risk coming back to warn them.

"He must really care about the Lucky Star horses," Sophie said, wiping the water from her eyes.

"A lot of people care," Shane said shortly. "They're a piece of history your grandparents have been preserving on this land."

"So let's go see if we can keep on preserving them!" Liv gave Cactus Jack a nudge and he took off after Temo.

"Slow," Shane warned. "We don't want to get there until everybody else is inside, and out of the rain."

Suddenly he stopped and looked around. "Where's Tux? Where's my dog?"

✳ ✳ ✳ ✳ ✳

"Tux hates thunder and lightning," said Shane as he paced the pine floor of the small barn where they'd found shelter. Like everything they'd been able to see through the rain as they rode up, the barn looked new and well-built, fitting the image of Silver Spur as a top guest ranch. "Darn dog probably took off at that first bolt of lightning," Shane went on. "We were too busy watching the black stallion to notice."

"But where would he go?" asked Liv.

Shane shrugged. "You know that dog. He has a mind of his own. Could be anywhere."

"He'll be okay," Sophie said, but she knew Shane was worried about Tux. She shivered with weariness, wet to the bone. When would they be able to leave? They'd been in the barn for hours; it was already getting dark outside. Their horses were stabled behind them, ready to go.

The door slid back at that moment and Temo appeared. "Glad you made it," he said. "Here are saddle blankets to warm the girls and some food from the kitchen."

He handled a bundle to Liv. "I can't stay," he said. "The other *vaqueros* are in the cookhouse, eating. They've separated Señor Starr's horses from the others and they're in the small corral right now. Do you have a plan to rescue them?"

Liv's hand brushed his as she took the bundle. Temo's hand was warm and rough and a tingle shot up her arm. "I — I don't think so," she stammered.

"Try," Temo urged. "And don't wait too long. I heard the *vaqueros* say they plan to load the horses around midnight. It is as we suspected, *amigos*. Señor Regis doesn't know you were there in the valley this afternoon. He plans to get the horses away before morning and tell Señor Starr that the black stallion took them away with him."

Shane was still pacing. "And once the horses are gone, there'll be no reason for your grandparents to hang onto that water hole. At least, that's the way Sam Regis thinks."

"But that's rustling!" Liv cried. "We have to do something, Shane."

"*Sí, muchacha*, you are right." Temo slid open the barn door. "But whatever you do — hurry!"

# CHAPTER 17
# Tux

Tux wriggled under the barn door at the Lucky Star ranch and shook himself to get rid of the water that soaked his shaggy coat. It had been a long run through the wind and rain.

A steady thudding came from Diego's stall. It was a different sound than before. The stallion was kicking not in frenzy but with steady determination. He wanted out.

Tux barked a greeting. He trotted, tail wagging, to the stall. Thud! Thud! Diego's hoofs hit the solid wood. Tux whined and stood on his hind legs, but he wasn't tall enough to see over the door. He dropped back to the floor, shook himself again and looked around. Like all dogs and horses, he could see in the dark. He tugged at a bale of straw near the stall, pulling the string with his teeth to get it nearer. It took a few tugs, but soon he was able to hop on the bale, stand on his back legs and look at Diego over the stall door.

Diego turned in the stall to see Tux's black and white face. The horse whickered and bobbed his big head. The two touched noses.

Then the big roan stallion wheeled around and kicked at the door again.

Tux whined and pawed at the stall latch. It was metal — a bolt that shot into a groove. Tux knew all about latches like this. In Shane's mobile home, he'd learned how to open the cupboard where the treats were stored. He worried the bolt with his teeth. It moved a little, but when Diego struck the door with a mighty kick, it slid back into place.

"Woof!" Tux barked, surprising Diego. He stopped kicking and turned to peer at Tux working the latch.

In less than a minute it was open and Tux barked again.

Diego nudged the door with his nose and it pushed against the straw bale. Tux hopped down. Diego gave a stronger shove and the stall door opened.

Sophie had left the main barn door open in her rush to escape on Cisco. Diego and Tux had nothing to stop them as they headed out to the rain swept ranch yard.

The wind brought the smell of his mares to Diego. He lifted his nose, bared his teeth and drew in their scent —

far away but definitely there. He was still hurting, still wounded and weak, but none of that mattered. He drank from a puddle of rainwater, jumped the fence and sped off in the darkness, whinnying to Tux to follow.

When they reached the entrance to Wild Horse Creek Canyon, Diego stopped. He sniffed again. Tux ran in front of him, barking. "Yip, yip!" Something was wrong. Both the animals sensed it. They turned away from the easy pass and started up the high, narrow path that led along the cliff face on the canyon wall.

✳ ✳ ✳ ✳ ✳

Back in the small barn at the Silver Spur Ranch, Shane, Liv and Sophie had gobbled down Temo's tacos filled with meat and beans, his milk and chocolate cookies. The three of them sat with their backs against the wall, wrapped in the saddle blankets Temo had brought them.

"How — how long should we wait?" Sophie was shivering with cold and exhaustion.

"Not too much longer," Shane said. "Till all ranch lights are out."

Finally, everything was quiet. Even the rain drumming on the roof had stopped. It was time to go. Sophie stood up and tested her ankle. It would hold her.

Cactus Jack, Cisco and Navajo were led from the barn. Outside, they could hear the Lucky Star horses moving in the corral to their left. The large horse transport trucks were parked behind the corral, just long box-like shapes in the dark.

Liv swung open the gate of the small corral so Shane

could ride inside on Navajo. "Close the gate and stay out of sight," Shane leaned down to tell her. "I'll get the horses in position and when I do, get ready to open it — fast!"

Sophie and Liv mounted Cactus Jack and Cisco. They stayed in the shadows of the hay barn, ready to race to open the gate and ride after Shane and the herd once they were streaming out of the corral.

But the Lucky Star horses were in no hurry to leave the safety of the enclosure. Spooked by the storm, the mares bunched up against the fence at the far end. When Shane pointed Navajo at the group, they split and ran in all directions. The dark shapes of the running mares and the smaller shapes of the foals flowed around him like black shadows. Even an experienced cutting horse like Navajo couldn't keep them together.

"It's like trying to herd water!" Liv hissed to Sophie.

At that moment, a light went on in the nearest bunkhouse. The milling horses had alerted the ranch house. Soon they heard running feet and shouts. "Something's riled up those mares," Sam Regis yelled. "Get over there and check on them."

Liv sucked in her breath. "They'll see Shane!" she hissed.

"Maybe not." Sophie pressed her arm. "Look —."
In the swirling commotion of horses, Shane had disappeared.

"What could've spooked 'em?" they could hear one of the ranch hands ask. "I wonder if that black mustang is still around, trying to break them out of the corral."

"Whatever it is, I'm not taking any chances," Sam Regis' shout answered. "Get these horses in the transports — NOW. I want them out of here, pronto."

"Sure, boss." There were shouts for other hands to come and help. Bright yard lights popped on. The corral gate was opened.

Liv gripped Sophie's hand. "Now they'll find Shane for sure."

Suddenly, Sophie and Liv heard hooves pounding over the rain-soaked earth, coming fast. A steel blue roan horse thundered between the two ranch hands at the gate, into the middle of the corral full of milling horses.

After him dashed a black and white dog.

"Diego!" whispered Sophie and Liv together. "Tux!"

Inside the corral, Shane, leaning off Navajo's side, scooped up a leaping Tux with one arm. Navajo sprinted for the gate.

"Hey there!" one of the ranch hands shouted. "Hold up!"

But Shane was through. Behind him, Diego was a frenzied fury of motion, snapping, wheeling, rounding up his mares and foals and heading them toward the gate. Sam Regis and the two Silver Spur hands scattered, scrambling out of the stallion's way.

In seconds it was all over. The herd, with Carmelita the lead mare in front and Diego in the rear, galloped toward their home range. Soon they had vanished in the darkness.

Shane pulled Navajo to a halt. Liv and Sophie rode out of the shadows into the glare of the yard lights.

Sam Regis stared at them, stunned. "What are you kids doing here?" His voice was like scraped gravel.

"We came to get our horses," Liv stepped forward. "The ones you stole."

Sam Regis' face turned red in the yard lights. "Be careful what you say," he growled. "That's a terrible thing, accusing folks of horse stealin'. I'll cut you girls some slack, cause I know you're not from around here but you — !" He pointed at Shane. "You should know better. But then you're most likely following Ted Starr's orders, aren't you? That old man's as crazy as a coot."

"We heard you," Sophie accused him. "You told the men to put the horses in trucks."

"You think I'd bother rustling Ted and Sandra Starr's precious Spanish colonials?" Sam gave a rough laugh. "Bah! These horses aren't worth nuthin' to me. They're practically wild."

He shrugged his wide shoulders. "I was going to do the neighborly thing and truck those mares and foals back to the Lucky Star Ranch, but if Diego wants to take them himself, he can be my guest." He turned on the heels of his fancy cowboy boots and stalked away, out of the lights.

His ranch hands shut the gate of the empty corral and followed.

Shane, Liv and Sophie stared after them.

"Can he just get away with those lies?" Liv's voice shook with anger.

"I guess so." Shane jammed his hat down on his head.

124

"He flat out denied he stole those horses and we can't prove he's lying. But we know the truth." He grinned and patted Liv's shoulder. "He stole 'em and it looks like Diego took him up on his offer to steal 'em back. We should go, too."

They rode off down the valley after Diego and his herd. When they'd put some distance between them and the Silver Spur Ranch, Shane halted long enough to lower his squirming dog to the ground. "Tux, you old cuss! Where did you come from, anyway?"

"And how did Diego get here?" Sophie stared in the direction the herd had vanished. "He was locked in his stall."

"Hard to say." Shane urged Navajo forward once more. "But I wouldn't be surprised if this fool dog had something to do with it."

# CHAPTER 18
# Flash Flood

They crossed the valley and rode up the ridge that separated it from Bobcat Canyon with Tux leading the way. At the top he barked and headed off to the right.

"What's wrong, Buddy?" Shane shouted. "No! We're not going up there."

"Where does he want to take us?" Sophie panted.

"Could be he wants to take the high trail along Wild Horse Creek Canyon." Shane shook his head. "Fool dog. Tux!" he shouted again. "Come here."

Sophie breathed a sigh of relief as they rode down the ridge. The thought of the narrow trail across the cliff face made her shudder.

"What an adventure!" Liv sang out as their horses scrambled and slid down the scree into Bobcat Canyon. "The lightning storm, the horses — the black stallion racing away over the desert and Diego appearing out of nowhere — I'll never forget this night as long as I live!

*Neither will I*! Sophie thought bitterly. Every jerk of Cisco's body sent a stab of pain shooting through her ankle.

Shane shot Liv an admiring glance. "You're quite a girl," he shouted. "Still lovin' all this action and ready for more after riding all day ..." He turned to look at Sophie. "But I think poor little Sophie is all worn out."

Poor little Sophie! That's how Shane would remember her! The kid who was scared of everything. The kid who couldn't keep up to her twin sister. If only people didn't compare her to Liv all the time!

Liv called back to her, "Don't worry, Sophie. It'll be easy from here on. All we have to do is ride back to the ranch."

"That's all?" Sophie could not stop the groan that escaped her.

"We'll just follow Diego's herd back through Wild Horse Creek Canyon," Liv went on cheerfully. "Horses can see in the dark and anyway, look! Here comes the moon."

A perfectly round moon soared up over the jagged peaks to the south, pale against the dark sky, lighting the floor of the canyon in front of them.

After a few minutes of moonlit riding, Shane pulled up on his horse and stared at the ground.

"What do you see?" Liv rode up beside him with Sophie bringing up the rear.

127

"Nuthin'." Shane checked the ground with flashlight from his saddlebag. "No tracks."

"Listen," Liv said. "Water!"

She was so disgustingly enthusiastic, Sophie thought bitterly. What was so thrilling about more water? They were all still wet from the thunderstorm.

"It's runoff from the storm," Shane told them. "The dry wash down the center of this canyon will be a regular river for an hour or two."

"Cool!" Liv exclaimed.

As they rode down the canyon, moonlight sparkled on the water.

At the fork, the rippling stream joined a rushing Wild Horse Creek. The large round stones in the creek bed tumbled over each other in the swift moving water, making loud music in the night.

"Diego and his herd will most likely be at the water hole," Shane called to Sophie and Liv. "We'll stop there and take a rest."

But when they reached the water hole, there was no sign of the herd. Shane rode around the brimming spring, searching the muddy ground, while Liv and Sophie slipped from their saddles.

"Is there something wrong?" asked Sophie anxiously.

"I don't understand," Shane replied, stowing his flashlight. "There's no fresh tracks or manure. Those horses haven't been here — something's the matter."

Tux whined up at him as if to say, "I told you so."

"I think Tux was trying to tell us the horses have taken the high trail."

"Why in the world would they do that?" asked Sophie.

"Maybe it's safer. That kind of storm we just had can create flash floods." Shane pointed to a cow trail that rose steeply to the switchbacks. "Sorry, Sophie, but I think the animals know more than we do. We should head for the heights."

Sophie could barely speak. The thought of riding that narrow ledge in the dark made her feel sick. "I don't think I can do it, Shane. What about the rattlesnakes?"

"It's too wet for them tonight. They won't be out on the trail sunnin' themselves like last time. C'mon. We'd better get goin'."

"Just lean forward as we climb," Liv said encouragingly as they set off up the cow path. "Cisco will know what to do. He's a Spanish horse — he can keep going."

Sophie threw her weight forward. They climbed upward through the moonlight, in and out of the shadows of the mesquite, up narrow, sandy channels between the rocks. She was suddenly aware of how carefully Cisco carried himself, balancing his body as he reached for the best footing. She loosened her grip on his reins, giving him his head.

They reached the switchbacks and above, Sophie saw Shane, already a whole level higher. "Hear that?" he called to them.

They heard a deep roar as though a powerful gust of wind was blowing toward them. "Here comes the flood," Shane shouted. "Good thing we're above it! Come on!"

Seconds later, a wall of water swept suddenly down the canyon, filling it from side to side, drowning the cow path they'd climbed.

Liv and Sophie did not look back. They followed Shane around another sharp bend and then another until they saw him reach the overhanging rock where Sophie had rested the day before. He stopped to let them catch up.

Below them, the flash flood snarled and bellowed like a wild thing, carrying branches, debris and whole trees with it. Huge boulders tumbled in the current, smashing against the canyon walls.

"Will the water come any higher?" Liv shouted ahead to Shane.

"Hard to say. We should keep going in case it does. When we get on the ledge, be careful — the rocks will be slippery with the rain. You okay, Sophie?"

"I think so."

"Good. Stay on your horses and let them find their own way. They can see and they know the trail."

*And they're not afraid of heights.* Sophie shuddered. The thought of crossing that cliff face was like returning to a horrifying nightmare.

# CHAPTER 19
# Cliff Face

They climbed the final switchbacks and set out across the slender ledge. Shane and Navajo disappeared around a corner of the rock. Navajo was faster than Cisco, who took his time placing his small hooves among the slippery rocks.

She heard Liv's voice behind her, sounding suddenly alarmed. "Sophie! Something's wrong with Cactus Jack. He's limping. I'm going to get off and see if I can see what's happened."

"No!" Sophie called back. "Shane told us to stay on our horses."

"But if it's just a stone in his hoof, maybe I can pry it loose."

"Don't get off!" Sophie turned to shout. "The trail's too narrow. Liv, stop!"

In the moonlight Sophie could see her twin slip from the wrong side of her saddle and squeeze between the cliff and Cactus Jack's body. His sore hoof must be on the outside of the ledge because Liv was crossing behind the horse and bending down.

As she picked up his hoof, Cactus Jack gave a sudden lurch.

Sophie heard Liv scream — saw her topple over the edge.

Time stopped. Breathing stopped. Sophie sat frozen on Cisco's back.

A small cry, barely audible above the raging water, came from below. "Sophie ... help!"

"Shane!" Sophie yelled but it was no use. He'd never hear over the thunder of the water sweeping down the canyon. She flung her leg over Cisco's back, slipped down his side and pressed herself against the wet cliff. Her sore ankle throbbed.

"Sophie, hurry!"

*I can't*, Sophie's brain shouted. *I can't move. I'm going to faint.* Her breath came in short puffs. *You have to,* a voice in her said. *Now.*

She took a step and then another, feeling her way along the cliff. When she got to Cactus Jack, she got down on her knees. She peered over the edge and felt sick again.

About fifteen feet below, Liv clung to the root of a dead pine tree with one arm. With the other, she hugged an outcrop of rock. Her boots scrabbled at the wet surface of the cliff, searching for a foothold. If she fell, she'd be swept away by the flood like the branches and the boulders.

"I think ... this rock's coming loose ..." Liv's voice sounded thin and childlike. The fear Sophie saw in Liv's face wiped out her own.

"Hold on," Sophie yelled.

*Remember your ski patrol training — find a rope,* she told herself. Cactus Jack had a lariat, a strong thin rope with a loop at one end for roping cattle, attached to his saddle. She would have to get it — stand up and get it.

Her heart pounded. She reached for Cactus Jack's reins which were dangling from his bridle. "Stand," she ordered him. "Don't move."

Using the reins, Sophie pulled herself to her feet. *Don't look down*, she told herself, *don't think about falling. Think about Liv*.

She undid the lariat from the saddle, found the loop and hooked it over Cactus Jack's saddle horn. The other end she wrapped around her waist and tied it in a strong knot. Now she had to look down.

She gasped. In the moonlight she could see that rain had loosened the soil around the rock. Mud fell on Liv's upturned face. She screamed again, "I'm going to fall!"

"Hold on!" Sophie said. "I'm coming."

She turned and faced the cliff and let herself over the edge. In one hand she held the coiled rope. With the other, she dug for a handhold, but there was only smooth, slippery sandstone.

She let herself down, swinging, until she was level with Liv's body. "I'm going to grab you," she said in a shaking voice. "You'll have to let go of the rock and hang onto me. NOW!"

She made a lunge for Liv. Liv's arms tightened around her. At that moment, the rock she had clung to let go. It rumbled down the cliff and splashed into the water far below.

Liv and Sophie swung in mid-air, clinging to each other. "Pull, Cactus Jack," Sophie shrieked.

Nothing happened. The lariat dug into Sophie's armpits.

"I can't ... hold on," she heard Liv whimper.

"I've got you, Liv. Don't give up," Sophie begged. At that moment she felt a tug on the rope from above and heard a voice shout. "I'm here!"

It was Shane! "Come on, Jack, GO!" he bellowed. Sophie felt the rope jerk — once, then again, and again.

She felt as though she was being torn in two. Cactus Jack hauled from above and Liv dragged on her waist. Then, suddenly she flopped on the ledge like a fish and Shane was reaching for Liv and Liv was lying beside her.

For a long moment they lay there, too breathless to speak. Then Liv reached out and found Sophie's hand.

Tux licked at the mud on Liv's face. She started to laugh and cry at the same time. "Thanks for the bath," she choked, sitting up.

Shane said, "Tux kept barking. I didn't realize you'd got so far behind ... that you were in trouble, but he made me go back."

"He's such a smart dog," Sophie said, sitting up and pressing her back against the cold, solid cliff. "And Cactus Jack's a fabulous cow horse. He pulled us both up the whole way."

"He can pull a thousand-pound bull if he has to." Shane stroked Cactus Jack's neck. "You were pretty good yourself," he went on, "for someone who hates heights." He bent down and gave her shoulder an awkward pat.

Sophie felt a burst of joy. "I still hate heights," she said with a laugh. "But I'm not afraid of them anymore. Let's get off this ledge and down on flat ground!"

Minutes later they were on their way. Liv rode in front of Sophie on Cisco with Sophie's arms wrapped around her waist. Shane followed, leading Cactus Jack who was too lame to be ridden. Soon this would all be over, Sophie thought. I'll go home and I'll probably never see Shane again. She glanced back at the lanky rider on his paint horse, picking his way down the canyon ledge. *I won't miss Wild Horse Creek Canyon*, she told herself, *but I'll never forget this night*.

# CHAPTER 20
# Mysteries

"That was mighty fast thinking, up there on the ledge," Shane shouted to Sophie as they rode back to the ranch. "How did you know what to do with the rope?"

Sophie shouted back, "Liv and I are in the junior ski patrol program. I don't enjoy patrolling, but it gives us a break on our tow fees." She wrapped her arms even tighter around Liv. "And now I'm really glad I had that training. It sort of takes over your brain in an emergency."

Liv gave her hand a squeeze. "You were amazing, that's all."

Minutes later, the Lucky Star Ranch barn loomed up, a black shape against the night sky.

"Look! Is that Diego and his whole herd?" Liv pointed to a large group of horses, grazing peacefully in the moonlight near the Lucky Star ranch gate.

"Yep," said Shane. "He brought them home." He hopped off Navajo to open the gate. "He knew they'd be safe here."

"But we still don't know how he got out of the barn," said Liv, as they rode into the ranch yard and slid wearily from their saddles.

They found part of the answer in the gaping barn door and the open door to Diego's stall.

"Maybe I didn't shut the main door when I left in a hurry, but this stall has been opened from the outside," Sophie said, fingering the bolt.

"Tux?" Liv looked down at the dog by Shane's side. "How did you do that?"

Tux jumped up on the bale of straw, cocked his head to one side and grinned his doggie grin as if to say, "Wouldn't you like to know!"

"That's not the only mystery," Sophie sighed. "What's happened to our mother? She should be back by now." She remembered her mother's voice on the message. Was there something she hadn't told them — something about Gran's tests?

✷ ✷ ✷ ✷ ✷

The message machine was blinking again when they trooped wearily into the ranch house, having fed and watered their three horses. Cactus Jack's lameness turned out to be a loose shoe. Once Shane had tapped in the loose nail he was ready to be turned out with the other horses for the night.

"It might be another message from Mom." Liv said, reaching for the phone. "What's the code?"

"It's *Lopez*," Sophie told her. "Gran's code."

Liv punched in the letters. The message crackled into the silence: "Hi, it's your mom. I'm on my way back now, but it looks like a storm's coming. Hope you kids are okay —" The message ended.

"Where is she?" Liv stared at Sophie and Shane. "She called hours ago."

"Try not to worry," Sophie said. "Come on, let's get into dry clothes, and I need you to bandage this ankle of mine. Shane, why don't you investigate the kitchen for food."

"Right!" Shane grinned at her. "I'm on it."

It was an hour later, after Sophie's ankle had been wrapped in an elastic bandage from their mom's nursing bag. Sophie and Liv had changed into dry clothes and found some of their Granddad's clothes for Shane, and the three of them had devoured the leftover steak and chocolate cake from last night's dinner. Tux had had his share, and then they heard their mom's van roll up to the ranch house so they ran out to meet her.

"The road was washed out." Jess enveloped Sophie and Liv in a bear hug. "It was scary! One minute there was a dry road, the next I was looking at this raging river.

I had to wait for the water to go down. Good thing you kids were here during the storm." She stared at them. "You were, weren't you?"

Liv and Sophie exchanged glances. No use telling Mom about what they'd been through — at least not yet. "We, uh, got a little wet," they admitted. "That's why Shane's wearing Granddad's clothes."

Jess turned to Shane. "Did you find Diego's mares?"

"They're over in the back pasture." Shane nodded.

"Great! And did the vet get here?" she went on, still with her arms around the twins' shoulders as they walked into the ranch house.

"He came ..." Sophie hesitated.

"Well — what did he say about Diego?" Jess asked as they stepped inside.

"I didn't actually meet him." Sophie hurried on, "but he fixed Diego up and he said he'd come back."

"That's good!" Jess collapsed on the cowhide couch and glanced at the phone. "Was there a message from your grandparents?"

"N-no," Liv said, but from the look on her mother's face she knew she was anxious to hear news from Tucson.

Shane said goodnight a few minutes later. He stood in the doorway with Tux by his side and looked shyly at Sophie. She could tell he wanted to hug her.

"What a day we had," she murmured, holding out her hand.

"Yes, we did." Shane shook it formally, up and down. He went on holding it a minute longer. "Guess I'll see you tomorrow. I'll ride over and check on Diego and Cactus Jack. Make sure we fixed Jack's shoe properly."

"That'll be good." Sophie nodded. "I'll see you tomorrow, then." She wished everyone wasn't watching. She wanted to hug Shane, too. Instead she smiled at him and gave a little shrug "Good night ..."

She watched him go until he'd crossed the ranch yard, then closed the door and turned back to the living room. Liv was yawning in her easy chair. "I'm ready for bed," she admitted. "Are you still going to sleep in Gran's room?"

Sophie stared at her. She'd forgotten all about it. "No," she blurted out. "I want you right where I can see you if I wake up in the night."

"Good," Liv sighed. "That's how I feel, too."

"Maybe I'll try the separate room thing some other time," Sophie said.

✳ ✳ ✳ ✳ ✳

The next morning the desert sparkled after the storm. Every dry leaf and cactus thorn had been washed clean of dust. The pure fresh air had the spicy tang of the desert.

Liv, Shane and Sophie sat on the fence overlooking the pasture where Diego and his herd grazed. Diego was once more the proud king. At the sound of a truck rolling toward the gate, he lifted his head and whinnied. He pawed at the ground with his foreleg and set off to circle his herd protectively.

"It's the Silver Spur Ranch truck!" Sophie jumped off the fence in surprise. "What are *they* doing here?"

Liv felt her heart thump. Temo was in the cab. She recognized his big black hat. The truck stopped at the gate and he swung out to open it, waving to them.

Dayna drove through without stopping and rolled the truck up beside the fence.

"She didn't even wait for Temo!" Liv said in disgust.

"I know," Sophie said. "She did the same thing yesterday. She's got the manners of a javelina. I don't even want to talk to her!" She ducked through the bars of the fence into the pasture.

Shane followed her. "Speaking of javelinas, how's your ankle this morning?"

"Better." Sophie said. "The swelling's almost gone. Puncture marks are better, too."

Shane shook his head and grinned. "You've *got* to try to take better care of yourself."

Meanwhile, Dayna had stepped from the truck cab and strolled over to Liv at the fence. She was wearing a bright red jacket with more fringe. "I see Diego's almost recovered," she said.

"Got his herd back, too," Liv couldn't help pointing out.

"Listen!" Dayna's chin shot up. "My father wasn't trying to round up your horses, especially. He was just trying to save *our* mares from that stray stallion. My father says that black horse will come back. He'll never

142

be content until he takes the herd away from Diego. He'll probably fight with Diego again and kill him if the ranchers don't do something."

Liv said nothing. It sounded as though Dayna was trying to convince herself that her father was a reasonable man, even if she didn't believe it.

Dayna reached in her pocket and pulled out an envelope. "This is an invitation to a free spa day at Silver Spur Ranch for you and your sister," she said with a toss of her head. "We offer it to all the newbies around here." She listed off the items: "The works — yoga, hot stones, massage, manicure, pedicure, make up, hair — tanning bed if you want it."

"Th-thanks," Liv stammered.

"And I'll invite the girls from the other ranches around," Dayna handed her the envelope with a flourish. "We'll have a party." She climbed through the fence rails and marched toward Shane and Sophie, with the fringe on her jacket swaying.

Liv looked at the envelope in her hand and sighed. If this was a peace offering, it was a good one — a chance to see the inside of the fancy guest ranch. A chance to see Temo again! But would Sophie agree to go?

Temo was striding toward her. "How are the *muchachas* this morning," he asked Liv.

"We're not kids!" Liv shot back before she could stop herself. It wasn't what she meant to say at all.

Temo threw back his head and laughed. "Well, you are

143

kids to me," he said, and then more seriously. "I heard what Diego did last night, rescuing his herd. What a horse, the best of his breed."

He touched Liv's arm lightly. "I hope he and the other horses can stay on this ranch," he said. "I hope your grandparents can hold onto it."

Liv gulped. There was a question she had to ask but it was hard with those wonderful brown eyes smiling at her. "If you care so much ... about the ranch and the horses ... why do you work for Mr. Regis?" she said. "Why do you do everything Dayna says?"

The smile disappeared from Temo's eyes. "It's not what I want." Temo's voice was low and urgent. "But my family works at the ranch. I have a cousin who is in the country illegally. It would be dangerous for him to return to Mexico —" he broke off. Dayna was walking back toward them.

" — so I hope you will be at the Lucky Star Ranch for a long time." Temo finished loud enough for her to hear.

"But we're not going to stay," Sophie said in a shocked voice. "We're going home in a week, when our grandparents get back."

# CHAPTER 21
# **Sophie Decides**

"When exactly *are* we leaving?" Sophie asked her mother that night at dinner.

"Well, we have to get you back for the first day of school," Jess said, "and it takes at least three days to drive to Vancouver. So I'd say Friday morning at the latest. I'll go to Tucson and pick up your grandparents Thursday."

Now that they had a definite time for going — Friday morning — Sophie started to enjoy certain things about the desert. She liked the way you could see the weather coming over the mountains.

She liked watching Diego and his mares and the foals.

Soon Wild Horse Creek would be dry enough for them to return to their home, but for now they spent their time near the ranch.

Most of all she liked Shane. She loved to watch him ride up on Navajo every morning, with Tux dashing ahead. She knew Shane thought of her as a little kid, the way Temo did, but that didn't stop the feelings she had watching him walking across the ranch yard with his easy stride, or sitting at the table, quietly listening, saying something only when it was important. She let herself dream whatever crazy dream about Shane she wanted, however romantic or reckless. Maybe he'd come to Vancouver some day. She'd show him the ocean — they'd go sea kayaking together, or whale watching.

Anything was possible because on Friday, *she was going home*.

✳ ✳ ✳ ✳ ✳

Liv was tortured by the thought of Friday. After Friday there would be no more desert mornings with the sun coming up over the mountains, spreading its rays across the hills. No more beautiful Spanish horses grazing in the dawn light, no more Cactus Jack!

Liv had come to love the sturdy chestnut the way she'd never loved another horse. He would greet her in the corral every morning with a bob of his head and a happy nicker, and Liv knew he thought she'd always be there with a bucket of water and some oats for him.

Cactus Jack was right. This was where she belonged!

On Wednesday night, the phone rang at six o'clock while they were eating dinner. Jess had cooked steaks again and made a cake, but nobody except Sophie felt much like eating.

Liv jumped up and ran for the phone. "Mom, it's Gran."

She watched her mother's face as she talked. Saw her wipe tears from her eyes as she walked slowly back to them.

"What's wrong?"

Jess sank down in the middle of the big cowhide sofa. "Liv, Sophie, come and sit with me," she murmured.

"Would you like me to leave, ma'am?" Shane asked quietly.

"No, I'd like you to stay." Jess wrapped one arm around Sophie and another around Liv. "I have some bad news about Gran," she said slowly. "I think all of us knew there were things she wasn't telling us about these tests she was having." She took a deep breath. "The doctors think she'll be fine, that's the most important thing. But she needs surgery right away and then, after she recovers, she'll need treatments for a few months."

Jess gulped. She looked from one stricken face to another, and then went on. "Gran is most worried about your granddad. Pop says he wants to stay up in Tucson for the surgery and then drive back and forth for the treatments so he can still look after the ranch. She thinks it's too much for him, and I agree. She wondered if we'd consider moving here for a few months and look after the ranch so they can both stay in Tucson."

Sophie said, "But we can't. We have to go back to school. You've got your job."

Jess waved her hands as if to clear the confusion. "I could get a leave of absence for six months. There are schools here, aren't there, Shane?"

"Yes, ma'am," Shane said. "There's a junior high school in Rattlesnake Bend."

"Go to school in Rattlesnake Bend?" Sophie rose from the sofa.

"It's not a bad school," Shane said quietly.

"I guess ... we'll have to stay, then." Sophie's voice shook. "I guess we're not going home."

Liv bit her lip. She could see what this decision had cost Sophie. There was a moment of silence. "Think about it overnight," Jess said at last. "I told your grandmother we'd let her know in the morning."

✳ ✳ ✳ ✳ ✳

Sophie lay awake most of the night, pictures filling her head. She saw the daffodils and forget-me-nots in her garden at home, the green grass of spring, the tall cedar and spruce trees surrounding their house in North Vancouver. She pictured English Bay with the ships riding at anchor — all pointing into the ocean wind. She saw Gran in the room downstairs, saying Sophie was welcome to sleep there while she was away, saw her in a hospital bed, away from the home she loved.

As the light in her window turned from black to gray, Sophie got up. She pulled on her socks, jeans and a sweatshirt, knowing the early morning would still be cold.

Outside, red lit the tops of the mountains to the east. A jackrabbit with huge ears loped across the ranch yard. She could hear the horses in the corral moving restlessly, waiting for their morning hay. Turning her back on the barn and the house, she followed the jackrabbit down the dirt lane toward the ranch gate and the open desert. The sun rose higher and light spilled over the mountains. The gray dawn light pulled back like a curtain.

Sophie stood still. Was she still in bed, asleep and dreaming? The dry earth blazed with color. The desert was a blanket of bright orange, purple and yellow flowers. She heard the clop of hoofs and saw Shane on Navajo, riding across the carpet of flowers. He had come early.

"Shane!" she shouted, running toward him. "What's happened? Am I dreaming?"

He rode closer. "Wildflowers," he said. "Poppies. Sometimes they bloom like this after a spring rain. Pretty, isn't it?"

"It's ... it's the most beautiful thing I've ever seen." Sophie gasped, "The whole desert's come to life."

"Oh, wait till you see the cactus in bloom," Shane said. "Even better. Each one's a different color." He looked down at her with his steady blue-gray eyes. "This place is full of surprises."

Sophie laughed. "Good thing I'm not leaving then, isn't it? The desert just sent me an invitation to stay."

A grin spread across Shane's thin face. "Hop up." He offered her a hand to hoist her on the saddle behind him. "We'll ride back in together."

✳ ✳ ✳ ✳ ✳

Wild Horse Creek was back between its banks, as Liv and Sophie rode through it the following Saturday on their way to the Silver Spur Ranch. Sophie had agreed to go, mainly to see Diego and his herd back in their home.

Only the damp earth along the creek, already caked and cracked from the heat, showed that there had ever been a flood.

"There they are!" Sophie cried. Diego stood on a high outcrop of rock, guarding his band of mares and foals. Diego's son, the blue roan foal with the bottlebrush tail, frisked up and down the creek bank.

"I'll bet that little fella will be a boss horse, just like his dad." Liv sighed dreamily. "Wouldn't it be wonderful to be here to watch him grow up?"

Sophie didn't answer. She knew that Liv imagined herself living on their grandparents' ranch, not just for a few months, but forever.

"Look at Diego," Liv went on. "He's standing right where that beautiful black stallion stood before the flood. Do you think Dayna's father is right? Will he come back and fight Diego for the herd?"

"We don't know what happened to the black stallion," Sophie said. "But if he's still out there, he might try."

"I hope they don't fight, but I'd love to see the *mestengo* again."

"So would I," Sophie admitted. She leaned forward to straighten Cisco's golden mane. "I'd love to see him flying like a phantom across the desert floor. I'd like to watch Diego's colt grow up to be a strong young yearling. And Shane says all the cacti are going to bloom this year after the rain —"

"And Gran will be back to tell us stories about the ranch in the old days when her great grandmother came from Mexico," Liv added.

"I know she will." Sophie nodded. Who knew what else the future would bring? A new school, new friends, new adventures. If she could rescue her sister from a dark cliff in Wild Horse Creek Canyon, anything was possible!